First published in Great Britain 2013
by Mills & Boon, an imprint of Harlequin (UK) Limited.
Harlequin (UK) Limited, Eton House, 18-24 Paradise Road,
Richmond, Surrey TW9 1SR

© Kate Hewitt 2013

ISBN: 978 0 263 23413 8

Harlequin (UK) policy is to use papers that are natural, renewable and recyclable products and made from wood grown in sustainable forests. The logging and manufacturing process conform to the legal environmental regulations of the country of origin.

Printed and bound in Great Britain
by CPI Antony Rowe, Chippenham, Wiltshire

IN THE HEAT OF
THE SPOTLIGHT

BY
KATE HEWITT

MILLS
BOON

IN THE HEAT OF
THE SPOTLIGHT

To my big brother Geordie, the real writer of Aurelie's song.
Thank you for always being my (tor)mentor. Love, K.

CHAPTER ONE

LUKE BRYANT STARED at his watch for the sixth time in the last four minutes and felt his temper, already on a steady simmer, start a low boil.

She was late. He glanced enquiringly at Jenna, his Head of PR, who made useless and apologetic flapping motions with her hands. All around him the crowd that filled Bryant's elegant crystal and marble lobby began to shift restlessly. They'd already been waiting fifteen minutes for Aurelie to make an appearance before the historic store's grand reopening and so far she was a no-show.

Luke gritted his teeth and wished, futilely, that he could wash his hands of this whole wretched thing. He'd been busy putting out corporate fires at the Los Angeles office and had left the schedule of events for today's reopening to his team here in New York. If he'd been on site, he wouldn't be here waiting for someone he didn't even want to see. What had Jenna been thinking, booking a washed-up C-list celebrity like Aurelie?

He glanced at his Head of PR again, watched as she bit her lip and made another apologetic face. Feeling not one shred of sympathy, Luke strode towards her.

'Where is she, Jenna?'

'Upstairs—'

'What is she doing?'

'Getting ready—'

Luke curbed his skyrocketing temper with some effort. 'And does she realise she's fifteen—' he checked his watch '—*sixteen* and a half minutes late for the one song she's meant to perform?'

'I think she does,' Jenna admitted.

Luke stared at her hard. He was getting annoyed with the wrong person, he knew. Jenna was ambitious and hardworking and, all right, she'd booked a complete has-been like Aurelie to boost the opening of the store, but at least she had a ream of market research to back up her choice. Jenna had been very firm about the fact that Aurelie appealed to their target group of eighteen to twenty-five-year-olds, she'd sung three chart-topping and apparently iconic songs of their generation, and was only twenty-six herself.

Apparently Aurelie still held the public's interest—the same way a train wreck did, Luke thought sourly. You just couldn't look away from the unfolding disaster.

Still, he understood the bottom line. Jenna had booked Aurelie, the advertising had gone out, and a significant number of people were here to see the former pop princess sing one of her insipid numbers before the store officially re-opened. As CEO of Bryant Stores, the buck stopped with him. It always stopped with him.

'Where is she exactly?'

'Aurelie?'

As if they'd been talking about anyone else. 'Yes. Aurelie.' Even her name was ridiculous. Her real name was probably Gertrude or Millicent. Or even worse, something with an unnecessary i like Kitti or Jenni. Either way, absurd.

'She's in the staff break room—'

Luke nodded grimly and headed upstairs. Aurelie had been contracted to sing and, damn it, she was going to sing. Like a canary.

Upstairs, Bryant's women's department was silent and empty, the racks of clothes and ghostly faceless mannequins seeming to accuse him silently. Today had to be a success. Bryant Stores had been slowly and steadily declining for the last five years, along with the economy. No one wanted overpriced luxuries, which was what Bryant's had smugly specialised in for the last century. Luke had been trying to change things for years but his older brother, Aaron, had insisted on having the final say and he hadn't been interested in doing something that, in his opinion, diminished the Bryant name.

When the latest dismal reports had come in, Aaron had finally agreed to an overhaul, and Luke just prayed it wasn't too late. If it was, he knew who would be blamed.

And it *would* be his fault, he told himself grimly. He was the CEO of Bryant Stores, even if Aaron still initialled many major decisions. Luke took responsibility for what happened in his branch of Bryant Enterprises, including booking Aurelie as today's entertainment.

He knocked sharply on the door to the break room. 'Hello? Miss…Aurelie?' *Why* didn't the woman have a last name? 'We're waiting for you—' He tried the knob. The door was locked. He knocked again. No answer.

He stood motionless for a moment, the memory sweeping coldly through him of another locked door, a different kind of silence. The scalding rush of guilt.

This is your fault, Luke. You were the only one who could have saved her.

Resolutely he pushed the memories aside. He shoved his shoulder against the door and gave it one swift and accurate kick with his foot. The lock busted and the door sprang open.

Luke entered the break room and glanced around. Clothes—silly, frothy, ridiculous outfits—were scattered across the table and chairs, some on the floor. And something else was on the floor.

Aurelie.

He stood there, suspended in shock, in memory, and then, swearing again, he strode towards her. She was slumped in the corner of the room, wearing an absurdly short dress, her legs splayed out like spent matchsticks.

He crouched in front of her, felt her pulse. It seemed steady, but what did he really know about pulses? Or pop stars? He glanced at her face, which looked pale and was lightly beaded with sweat. Actually, now that he looked at her properly, she looked awful. He supposed she was pretty in a purely objective sense, with straight brownish-blonde hair and a lithe, slender figure, but her face was drawn and grey and she looked way too thin.

He touched her cheek and found her skin clammy. He reached for his cell phone to dial 911, his heart beating far too hard. She must have overdosed on something. He'd never expected to see this scenario twice in one lifetime, and the remembered panic iced in his veins.

Then her eyes fluttered open and his hand slackened on the phone. Luke felt something stir inside him at the colour of her eyes. They were slate-blue, the colour of the Atlantic on a cold, grey day, and they swirled with sorrow. She blinked blearily, struggled to sit up. Her gaze focused in on him and something cold flashed in their blue depths. 'Aren't you handsome,' she mumbled, and the relief he felt that she was okay was blotted out by a far more familiar determination.

'Right.' He hauled her up by the armpits and felt her sag helplessly against him. She'd looked thin slumped on the floor, and she felt even more fragile in his arms. Fragile and completely out of it. 'What did you take?' he demanded. She lolled her head back to blink up at him, her lips curving into a mocking smile.

'Whatever it was, it was a doozy.'

Luke scooped her up in his arms and stalked over to the bathroom. He ran a basin full of cold water and in one quick and decisive movement plunged the pop star's face into the icy bowlful.

She came up like a scalded cat, spluttering and swearing. 'What the *hell*—?'

'Sobered up a bit now, have you?'

She sluiced water from her face and turned to glare at him with narrowed eyes. 'Oh, yes, I'm sober. Who are you?'

'Luke Bryant.' He heard his voice, icy with suppressed rage. Damn her for scaring him. For making him remember. 'I'm paying you to perform, princess, so I'll give you five minutes to pull yourself together and get down there.' She folded her arms, her eyes still narrowed, her face still grey and gaunt. 'And put some make-up on,' Luke added as he turned to leave. 'You look like hell.'

Aurelie Schmidt—not many people knew about the Schmidt—wiped the last traces of water from her face and blinked hard. Stupid man. Stupid gig. Stupid her, for coming today at all. For trying to be different.

She drew in a shuddering breath and grabbed a chocolate bar from her bag. Unwrapping it in one vicious movement, she turned to stare at the clothes scattered across the impromptu dressing room. Jenna, the Bryant stooge who had acted as her handler, had been horrified by her original choice of outfit.

'But you're *Aurelie*… You have an *image*…'

An image that was five years past its sell-by date, but people still wanted to see it. They wanted to see her, although whether it was because they actually liked her songs or just because they hoped to see her screw up one more time was open to debate.

And so she'd forsaken the jeans and floaty top she'd been wanting to wear and shimmied into a spangly minidress instead. She'd just been about to do her make-up when she must have passed out. And Mr Bossy Bryant had come in and assumed the worst. Well, she could hardly blame him. She'd done the worst too many times to get annoyed when someone jumped to that rather obvious conclusion.

Clearly she was late, so she wolfed down her chocolate bar and then did the quick version of her make-up: blush, concealer, eyeliner and a bold lipstick. Her hair looked awful but at least she could turn it into a style. She pulled it up in a messy up-do and sprayed it to death. People would like seeing her a little off her game anyway. It was, she suspected, why they were here; it was why the tabloids still rabidly followed her even though she hadn't released a single in over four years. Everyone wanted to see her fail.

It had been a good twenty minutes since she was meant to perform her once-hit single *Take Me Down*, and Aurelie knew the audience would be getting restless. And Luke Bryant would be getting even more annoyed. Her lips curved in a cynical smile as she turned to leave the break room. Luke Bryant obviously had extremely low expectations of her. Well, he could just join the club.

Stepping onto a stage—even a makeshift one like this—always felt like an out-of-body experience to Aurelie. Any sense of self fell away and she simply became the song, the dance, the performance. Aurelie as the world had always known her.

The crowd in front of her blurred into one faceless mass and she reached for the mike. Her stiletto heel caught in a gap in the floor of the stage and for a second she thought she was going to pitch forward. She heard the sudden collective intake of breath, knew everyone was waiting, even hoping, she'd fall flat on her face. She righted herself, smiled breez-ily and began to sing.

Usually she wasn't aware of what she was doing onstage. She just did it. Sing, slink, shimmy, smile. It was second nature to her now, *first* nature, because performing—being someone else—felt far easier than being herself. And yet right there in the middle of all that fakery she felt something inside her still and go silent, even as she sang.

Standing on the side of the makeshift stage, away from the audience assembled in the lobby, Luke Bryant was star-ing right at her, his face grim, his eyes blazing. And worse, far worse, since he *should* be staring at her, was the reali-sation that she was staring back at him. And some part of herself could not look away even as she turned back to face the crowd.

Luke watched as Aurelie began her routine, and knew that was what it was. She was on autopilot, but she was good enough that it didn't matter. Her whipcord-slender body moved with an easy, sensual grace. Her voice was clear and true but also husky and suggestive when she wanted it to be, like sunshine and smoke. It was a sexy voice, and she was good at what she did. Even annoyed as he was with her, he could acknowledge that.

And then she turned and looked at him, and any smug sense of detachment he felt drained away. All he felt was... *need*. An overwhelming physical need for her but, more than that, a need to...to *protect* her. How ridiculous. He didn't even like her; he *despised* her. And yet in that still, silent second when their gazes met he felt a tug of both heart and... well, the obvious.

Then she looked away and he let out a shuddering breath, relieved to have that weird reaction fade away. Clearly he was overtired and way too stressed, to be feeling like that about someone like Aurelie. Or anyone at all.

He heard her call out to the crowd to sing along to the chorus of the admittedly catchy tune, and watched as she tossed her head and shouted, 'Come on, it's not that old a hit that you can't remember!'

He felt a flicker of reluctant admiration that she could make fun of herself. It took courage to do that. Yet remembering her slumped on the break room floor made his mouth twist down in disapproval. Dutch courage, maybe. Or worse.

The music ended, three intense minutes of song and dance, and Luke listened to the thunder of applause. He heard a few catcalls too and felt himself cringe. They liked her, but part of liking her, he knew, was making fun of her. He had a feeling Aurelie knew that too. He watched as she bowed with a semi-sardonic flourish, fluttered her fingers at her fans and sashayed offstage towards him. Their gazes clashed once more and Aurelie tipped her chin up a notch, her eyes flashing challenge.

Luke knew he'd treated her pretty harshly upstairs, but he wasn't about to apologise. The woman might have been on *drugs*. Now that she had done her act he wanted her out of here. She was way too much of a wild card to have in the store today. She came towards him and he reached out and curled one hand around her wrist.

He felt the fragility of her bones under his fingers, the frantic hammering of her pulse, and wished he hadn't touched her. Standing so close to her, he could smell her perfume, a fresh, citrusy scent, feel the heat from her body. He couldn't quite keep his gaze from dipping down to the smooth roundness of her breasts and the gentle flaring of her hips, outlined all too revealingly under the thin, stretchy material of her skimpy dress. His gaze travelled back up her body and he saw her looking at him with an almost weary cynicism.

He dropped her wrist, conscious that he'd just given her a very thorough once-over. 'Thank you,' he said, and heard how stiff his voice sounded.

Her mouth twisted. 'For what, exactly?'

'For singing.' He hated the lilt of innuendo in her voice.

'No problem, Bossy.'

Annoyance flared. 'Why do you think I'm bossy?'

'We-ell...' She put her hands on her hips. 'You dunked me in a sink of cold water and expected me to thank you for it.'

'You were passed out. I was doing you a favour.'

Her lips curved and her eyes glittered. Everything about her mocked him. 'See what I mean?'

'I just want you to do what you're meant to do,' Luke said tightly. The sooner this woman was out of here, the better. The store opening didn't need her. He didn't need her.

With that same mocking smile she placed one slender hand on his chest so he could see her glittery nail varnish—and she could feel the sudden, hard thud of his heart. He could feel the heat of her hand through his shirt, the gentle press of her slender fingers and, irritatingly, his libido stirred.

'And what,' she asked, her voice dropping an octave, 'am I meant to do?'

'Leave,' he snapped. He couldn't control his body's reaction, much as he wanted to, but he could—and would—control everything else.

She just laughed softly and pressed her hand more firmly against the thin cotton of his shirt, spreading her fingers wide. He remained completely still, stony-faced, and she dropped her gaze downwards. 'You sure about that?' she murmured.

Fury beat through his blood and he picked up her hand—conscious again of its slender smallness—and thrust it back at her as if it were some dead thing. 'I'll have security escort you out.'

She raised her eyebrows. 'And that will look good on today of all days.'

'What do you mean?'

'Having Aurelie escorted out by your security buffoons? The tabloids will eat it up with a spoon.' She folded her arms, a dangerous glitter in her eyes. It almost looked as if she was near tears or, more likely, triumph. 'Your big opening will be made into a mockery. Trust me, I know how it goes.'

'I have no doubt you do.' She'd been ridiculed in the press more times than he cared to count.

'Suck it up, Bossy,' she jeered softly. 'You need me.'

Luke felt his jaw bunch. And ache. He was tempted to stand his ground and tell her to leave, but rationality won out. Too much rode on this event to stand on stupid pride. 'Fine,' he said evenly. 'You can circulate and socialise for an hour, and then leave of your own accord. But if you so much as—'

'What?' She raised her eyebrows, her mouth curving into another mocking smile. 'What do you think I'm going to do?'

'That's the problem. I have absolutely no idea.'

She'd looked so coy and cat-like standing there, all innuendo and outrageous suggestion, but suddenly it was as if the life had drained out of her and she looked away, her expression veiled, blank. 'Don't worry,' she said flatly. 'I'll give everyone, even you, what they want. I always do.' And without looking back at him she walked towards the crowd.

Watching her, Luke felt a flicker of uneasy surprise. He'd assumed Aurelie was as shallow as a puddle, but in that moment when she'd looked away he'd sensed something dark and deep and even painful in her averted gaze.

He let out a long, low breath and turned in the opposite direction. He wasn't going to waste another second of his time thinking about the wretched woman.

Now that the mini-concert was over, the crowd milled around, examining the glass display cases of jewellery and make-up, the artful window dressings. Luke forced himself to focus on what lay ahead. Yet even as he moved through the crowd, smiling, nodding, talking, it seemed as if he could still feel the heat of her hand on his chest, imagined that its imprint remained in the cloth, or even on his skin.

Aurelie turned around to watch Luke Bryant walk away, wondering just what made Mr Bossy tick. He was wound tight enough to snap, that was for sure. When she'd placed her hand on his chest she'd felt how taut his muscles were, how tense. And she'd also felt the sudden thud of his heart, and knew she affected him. Aroused him.

The knowledge should have given her the usual sense of grim satisfaction, but it didn't. All she felt was tired. So very tired, and the thought of performing on a different kind of stage, playing the role of Aurelie the Pop Star for another hour or more, made her feel physically sick.

What would happen, she wondered, if she dropped the flirty, salacious act for a single afternoon, stopped being Aurelie and tried being herself instead?

She thought of the PR lady's look of horror at such a suggestion. No one wanted Aurelie the real person. They wanted the pop princess who tripped through life and made appalling tabloid-worthy mistakes. That was the only person they were interested in.

And that was the only person she was interested in being. She wasn't even sure if there was anything left underneath, inside. Taking a deep breath, she squared her shoulders and headed into the fray.

The crowd mingling in the elegant lobby of Bryant's was a mix of well-heeled and decidedly middle class. Aurelie had known Bryant's as a top-of-the-line, big-name boutique but, from a glance at the jewellery counter, she could tell the reopening was trying to hit a slightly more affordable note.

She supposed in this economy it was a necessary move and, from her quick once-over, it didn't seem that the store had sacrificed style or elegance in its pursuit of the more price-conscious shopper. Ironic, really, that both she and Bryant's were trying to reinvent themselves. She wondered if Luke would make a better job of it than she had.

For three-quarters of an hour she worked the crowd, signing autographs and fluttering her fingers and giggling and squealing as if she was having the time of her life. Which she most certainly was not. Yet even as she played the princess, she found her gaze wandering all too often to Luke Bryant. From the hard set of his jaw and the tension in his shoulders, he looked as if he wasn't having the time of his life, either. And, unlike her, he wasn't able to hide it.

He was certainly good-looking enough, with the dark brown hair, chocolate eyes and powerful body she remembered the feel of. Yet he looked so serious, so stern, his dark eyes hooded and his mouth a thin line. Did he ever laugh or even smile? He'd probably had his sense of humour surgically removed.

Then she remembered the thud of his heart under her hand and how warm his skin had felt, even through the cotton of his shirt. She remembered how he'd looked down at her, first with disapproval and then with desire. Typical, she told herself, yet something in her had responded to that hot, dark gaze, something in her she'd thought had long since died.

His gaze lifted to hers and she realised she'd been staring at him for a good thirty seconds. He stared back in that even, assessing way, as if he had the measure of her and found it decidedly lacking. Aurelie felt her heart give a strange little lurch and deliberately she let her gaze wander up and down his frame, giving him as much of a once-over as he'd given her. His mouth twisted in something like distaste and he turned away.

Aurelie stood there for a moment feeling oddly rebuffed, almost hurt. How ridiculous; all she'd been trying to do was annoy him. Besides, she'd suffered far worse insults than being dismissed. All she had to do was open a newspaper or click on one of the many celebrity gossip sites. Still, she couldn't deny the needling sense of pain, like a splinter burrowing into her heart. Why did this irritating man affect her so much, or even at all?

She heard the buzz of conversation around her and tried to focus on what someone was saying. Tried to smile, to perform, yet somehow the motions wouldn't come. She was failing herself, and in one abrupt movement she pivoted on her heel and walked out of the crowded lobby.

Luke watched Aurelie leave the lobby and felt an irritating mix of satisfaction and annoyance war within him. He didn't particularly want the woman around, yet he hadn't liked the look on her face, almost like hurt, when he'd gazed back at her. Why he cared, he had no idea. He *didn't* care. He wanted her gone.

And yet he could remember the exact blue-grey shade of her eyes, saw in that moment how they had darkened with pain. And despite every intention to stay and socialise, he found himself walking upstairs, back to the break room where he figured Aurelie had gone.

He pushed open the now-broken door without knocking, stopping suddenly when he saw Aurelie inside, in the process of pulling her dress over her head.

'Excuse me—'

'No need to be shy, boss man.' She turned around wearing nothing but a very skimpy push-up bra and thong, her hands on her hips, eyebrows raised, mouth twisted. 'Now you can have the good look you've been wanting.'

He shook his head. 'You're really unbelievable.'

'Why, that's almost a compliment.'

And Luke knew he *was* having a good look. Again. He could not, to his shame, tear his gaze away from those high, firm breasts encased in a very little bit of white satin. Furious with himself, he reached for a gauzy purple top lying on the floor and tossed it to her. 'Put something on.'

She glanced at the top and her mouth curled in a feline smile. 'If you insist.'

She didn't look any more decent in the see-through top. In fact, Luke decided, she looked worse. Or better, depending on your point of view. The diaphanous material still managed to highlight the slender curves that had been on such blatant display. She was too skinny, he told himself, yet once again he could not keep his gaze from roving over her body, taking in its taut perfection. He felt another stirring of arousal, much to his annoyance. Aurelie's mouth curved in a knowing smile.

'I came up here,' he finally bit out, 'to see if you were all right.'

She raised her eyebrows, and he sensed her sudden tension. 'And why wouldn't I be all right?'

'Because—' What could he say? *Because I saw such sadness in your eyes.* He was being ridiculous. About a completely ridiculous woman. 'You seemed troubled,' he finally answered, because he didn't dissemble or downright lie. He wouldn't, not since that moment twenty-five years ago when he'd put his heart and soul on the line and hadn't been believed.

'Troubled?' Her voice rang out, incredulous, scornful. Yet he still saw those shadows in her eyes, felt the brittleness of her confident pose, hands on hips, chin—and breasts— thrust out. She cocked her head, lashes sweeping downwards. 'Aren't you Mr Sensitive,' she murmured, her voice dropping into husky suggestion that had the hairs on the back of

Luke's neck prickling even as his libido stirred insistently. It had been far too long since he'd been in a relationship. Since he'd had sex. That had to be the only reason he was reacting to this woman at all.

She sashayed towards him, lifted her knowing gaze to his. Luke took an involuntary step backwards, and came up against the door. 'I think you're the troubled one, Mr Bossy,' she said, and with a cynical little smile she reached down to skim the length of his burgeoning erection with her fingertips. Luke felt as if he'd been jolted with electricity. He stepped back, shook his head in disgust.

'What is *wrong* with you?'

'Obviously nothing, judging by your reaction.'

'If I see a fairly attractive woman in her underwear, then yes, my body has a basic biological reaction. That's all it is.'

'Oh, so your little show of concern for my emotional state was just that?' She stepped back, and her smile was now cold, her eyes hard.

'You think I was coming on to you?' He let out a short, hard laugh. 'If anything, you're the one who's been coming on to me. I don't even like you, lady.'

She lifted her chin, her eyes still hard. 'Since when did like ever come into it?'

'It does for me.'

'How quaint.' She turned away and, reaching for a pair of jeans, pulled them on. 'Well, you can breathe a sigh of relief. I'm fine.'

And even though he knew he should leave—hell, he should never have come up here in the first place—Luke didn't move. She didn't *seem* fine.

He stood there in frustration—sexual frustration now, too—as Aurelie piled all the clothes scattered around the room into a big canvas holdall. She glanced up at him, those stormy eyes veiled by long lashes, and for a second, no more, she looked young. Vulnerable. Then she smiled—he hated that cold, cynical smile—and said, 'Still here, Bossy? Still hoping?'

'I'm here,' he said through gritted teeth, remembrance firing his fury, 'because you're a complete disaster and I can't trust you to walk out of here on your own two feet. An hour ago you were passed out on the floor. The last thing I need is some awful exposé in a trashy tabloid about how pop princess Aurelie ODed in the break room.'

She rolled her eyes. 'Oh, and here I was, starting to believe you were actually *concerned* about me. Don't worry, I told you, I'm fine.'

Luke jerked his head into the semblance of a nod. 'Then I'll say goodbye and thank you to use the back door on your way out.'

'I always do. Paparazzi, you know.' She smiled, but he saw her chin tremble, just the tiniest bit, and with stinging certainty he knew that despite her go-to-hell attitude, he'd hurt her.

And even though he knew he shouldn't care, not one iota, he knew he did. 'Goodbye,' he said, because the sooner he was rid of her, the better. She didn't answer, just stared at him with those storm cloud eyes, her chin lifted defiantly—and still trembling. Swearing aloud this time, Luke turned and walked out of the room.

CHAPTER TWO

"'BRYANT'S REOPENING HIT exactly the right note between self-deprecation and assurance,'" Jenna read from the newspaper as she came into Luke's office, kicking the door closed behind her with one high-heeled foot. She glanced at him over the top of the paper, her eyes dancing. 'It was a total hit!'

Luke gave a rather terse smile back. He didn't want to kill Jenna's buzz, but he hadn't meant the reopening to be 'self-deprecating'—whatever that was supposed to mean. A quick scan of the morning's headlines had reassured him that the opening had been well received, if not exactly how he'd envisioned, and the till receipts at the end of the day had offered more proof. It was enough, Luke hoped, to continue the relaunch of Bryant Stores across the globe—if his brother Aaron agreed.

He felt the familiar pang of frustration at still having to clear any major decisions with his brother, even though he was thirty-eight years old and had been running Bryant Stores for over a decade. He'd surely earned a bit more of Aaron's trust, but his brother never gave it. Their father had set up the running of Bryant Enterprises in his will, and it meant that Aaron could call all the shots. And that, Luke knew, was one thing Aaron loved to do.

'Getting Aurelie really worked,' Jenna said. 'All the papers mention her.'

'They usually do,' Luke answered dryly. He spun around in his chair to face the rather uninspiring view of Manhattan's midtown covered in a muggy midsummer haze. He did *not* want to think about that out-of-control pop princess, or the shaming reaction she'd stirred up in him.

'Apparently it was a stroke of genius to have her sing,' Jenna continued, her voice smug with self-satisfaction.

'Hitting the right note between self-deprecation and assurance?' Luke quoted. The newspaper had managed to ridicule Aurelie even as they lauded the opening. *Even if Aurelie is too washed up to reinvent herself, Bryant's obviously can.* Briefly he closed his eyes. How did she stand it, all the time? Or did she just not care?

'Maybe you should have her perform at all the openings,' Jenna suggested and Luke opened his eyes.

'I don't think so.'

'Why not?' Jenna persisted. 'I know she's a bit of a joke, but people still like her music. And the newspapers loved that we hired a has-been to perform… They thought it was an ironic nod to—'

'Our own former celebrity. Yes, I read the papers, Jenna. I'm just not sure that was quite the angle we were going for.' Luke turned around and gave his Head of PR a quelling look. He liked hiring young people with fresh ideas; he wanted change and innovation, unlike his brother. But he didn't want Aurelie.

Actually, the problem is, you do.

'Maybe not,' Jenna persisted, 'but it worked. And the truth is that nobody wants the old Bryant's any more. You can only coast on a reputation for so long.'

'Tell that to Aurelie,' he said, meaning to close down the conversation, but Jenna let out a sharp little laugh.

'But that's all she has. Do you know she actually wanted

to sing something new—some soppy folk ballad.' Jenna rolled her eyes, and Luke stilled.

'A *folk* ballad? She's a pop star.'

'I know, ridiculous, right? I don't know *what* she was thinking. She wanted to wear jeans, for heaven's sake, and play her *guitar*. Like we hired her for that.'

Luke didn't answer, just let the words sink in. 'What did you say to her?' he asked after a moment.

'I told her we'd hired her to be Aurelie, not Joan Baez.'

He rolled a silver-plated pen between his fingers, his gaze resting once more on the hazy skyline. 'What did she say?'

Jenna shrugged. 'Not much. We're the ones who hired her. What could she do, after all?'

Nothing, Luke supposed. Nothing except lash out at anyone who assumed she was just that, only that—Aurelie, the shallow pop princess. An uncomfortable uncertainty stole through him at the thought.

Who *was* Aurelie, really?

'That will be all, Jenna,' he said and, looking faintly miffed since he'd always encouraged a spirit of camaraderie in the office, she left. Luke sank back into his chair and rubbed his hands over his face.

He didn't want to think about Aurelie. He didn't want to wonder if there was more to her than he'd ever expected, or worry about what she must have been feeling. He didn't want to think about her at all.

Sighing, he dropped his hands to stare moodily out of the window. Jenna's suggestion was ridiculous, of course. There was absolutely no way he was hiring Aurelie to open so much as a sugar packet for him. He never wanted to see her again.

Then why can't you get her eyes out of your mind?

Her eyes. When he closed his own, he saw hers, stormy and sad and *brave*. He was being ridiculous, romantic, and about a woman whose whole lifestyle—values, actions, ev-

erything—he despised. She might have written some soppy
new song, but it didn't change who she was: a washed-up,
over-the-top diva.

Yet her eyes.

He let out a groan of frustration and swivelled back to
face his computer. He didn't need this. The reopening of the
New York flagship store might have been a success, but he
still had a mountain of work to do. Bryant Enterprises had
over a hundred stores across the world and Luke intended
to overhaul every single one.

Without the help of Aurelie.

Aurelie bit her lip in concentration as she played the four
notes again. Did it sound too melancholy? She had to get
the bridge right or—

Or what?

She glanced up from the piano to stare unseeingly around
the room she'd converted into a work space. Nobody wanted
her music any more. She might be good for rehashing a few
of her hit singles, but nobody wanted to hear soulful piano
and acoustic guitar ballads. She'd got that loud and clear.

When she'd stupidly mentioned such an idea to her agent,
he'd laughed. *Laughed.* 'Stick with what you're good at,
babe,' he'd said. 'Not that it's all that much.'

She'd fired him. Not that it mattered. He'd been about to
let her go anyway.

Sighing, she rose from the piano bench and went to the
kitchen. She'd been working all morning and it was time for a
coffee break. She hated indulging in self-pity; she knew there
was no point. She'd made her bed and she'd spend the rest of
her life lying in it. No one was going to let her change. And,
really, she didn't need to change. At least not publicly. She
could spend the rest of her life living quietly in Vermont. She
didn't need a comeback, despite her pathetic attempt at one.

Just the memory of the Bryant's booking made her cringe. The only reason she'd accepted it was to have a kind of test run, to see how people responded to a new and different Aurelie. And it had failed at the very first gate. The Head of PR who had booked her had been appalled by her suggestion she do something different. *People are coming to see the Aurelie they know and love, not some wannabe folk singer. We only want one thing from you.*

Sighing again, she poured herself a coffee and added milk, stirring moodily. She'd given them the old Aurelie, just as that woman had wanted. She'd given it to them in spades. Briefly she thought of bossy Luke Bryant, and how she'd baited him. Even now she felt a flicker of embarrassment, even shame. All right, yes, she'd seen the desire flaring in his eyes, but instead of ignoring it she'd wound him up on purpose. She'd just been, as always, reacting. Reacting to the assumptions and sneers and suggestions. When she was in the moment it was so incredibly hard to rise above it.

The doorbell rang, a rusty croak of a sound, surprising her. She didn't get visitors. The paparazzi didn't know about this house and the townspeople left her alone. Then she remembered she'd ordered a new capo, and went to answer it.

'Hey…' The word died off to nothing as she stared at the man standing on the weathered front porch of her grandma's house. It wasn't the postman. It was Luke Bryant.

Luke watched the colour drain from Aurelie's face as she stared at him, obviously shocked. As shocked as he had been when he'd found this place, for an old farmhouse in a sleepy town in Vermont was not what he'd expected at all. He'd supposed it was a pretty good cover for someone like her, but it had only taken about ten seconds standing on her front porch to realise this wasn't a bolt-hole. It was home.

'What...' She cleared her throat, staring at him with wide, dazed eyes. 'What are you doing here?'

'Looking for you.'

'Why?' She sounded so bewildered he almost smiled. Gone was any kind of innuendo, any flirt. Gone, in fact, was so much as a remnant of the Aurelie he'd encountered back in New York. He looked at her properly for the first time, and knew he wouldn't have even recognised her if not for the colour of her eyes. He'd remembered those straight off. The woman in front of him was dressed in faded jeans and a lavender T-shirt, her silky hair tossed over one shoulder in a single braid. She wore no make-up, no jewellery. She was the essence of simplicity and, despite the slight gauntness of her face and frame, Luke thought she looked better now than he'd ever seen her in person or on an album cover.

'May I come in?'

'I...' She glanced behind her shoulder, and Luke wondered what she was hiding. Suspicion hardened inside him. All right, the house might be quaint in a countrified kind of way, and her clothes were...well, normal, but could he really doubt that this woman was still the outrageous, unstable pop star he'd met before?

Well, yes, he could.

He'd been doubting it, aggravatingly, ever since Jenna had suggested he book her for a string of openings and he'd refused. Refused point-blank even as he couldn't get her out of his mind. Those eyes. That sense of both sadness and courage. And how she must have come to Bryant's wanting to be different.

That was what had finally made him decide to talk to her. What a coup it would be to have Bryant's orchestrate a comeback for a has-been pop star that no one believed could change.

Although if he were honest—which he was determined

always to be—it wasn't the success of the store that had brought him to Vermont. It was something deeper, something instinctive. He understood all too well about wanting to change, trying to be different. He'd been trying with the store for nearly a decade. And as for himself... Well, he'd had his own obstacles to overcome. Clearly Aurelie had hers.

Which had brought him here, five weeks later, to her doorstep.

'May I come in?' he asked again, politely, and she chewed her lip, clearly reluctant.

'Fine,' she finally said, and moved aside so he could enter.

He stepped across the threshold, taking in the overflowing umbrella stand and coat rack, the framed samplers on the walls, the braided rug. Very quaint. And so not what he'd expected.

She closed the door and kept him there in the hall, her arms folded. 'How did you find me?'

'It was a challenge, I admit.' Aurelie had been off the map. No known address besides a rented-out beach house in Beverly Hills, no known contacts since her agent and manager had both been fired. Jenna had contacted her directly through her website, which had since closed down.

'Well?' Her eyes sparked.

'I'm pretty adept with a computer,' Luke answered. 'I found a mention of the sale of this house from a Julia Schmidt to you in the town property records.' She shook her head, coldly incredulous, and he tried a smile. 'Aurelie Schmidt. I wondered what your last name was.'

'Nice going, Sherlock.'

'Thank you.'

'I still don't know why you're here.'

'I'd like to talk to you.'

She arched an eyebrow, smiled unpleasantly. 'Oh? That wasn't the message you were sending me back in New York.'

'That's true. I'm sorry if I appeared rude.'

'Appeared? Well, I *appeared* like I was strung out on drugs, so what does it really matter?' She pivoted on her heel and walked down a dark, narrow hall, the faded wallpaper cluttered with photographs Luke found he longed to look at, to the kitchen.

'Appeared?' he repeated as he stood in the doorway, sunlight spilling into the room from a bay window that overlooked a tangled back garden. Aurelie had picked up a mug of coffee and took a sip. She didn't offer him any.

'I told you, it doesn't matter.'

'Actually, it does. If you have a substance abuse problem, I need to know about it now.' That was the one thing that had almost kept him from coming at all. He would not work with someone who was unstable, who might overdose. He would never put himself in that position again.

'You need to know?' she mocked. She held her coffee mug in front of her as if it was some kind of shield, or perhaps a weapon. Luke stayed by the door. He didn't want its contents thrown in his face. 'What else do you *need*, Luke Bryant?'

Her eyes flashed and he tensed. He hated innuendo, especially when he knew it held a shaming grain of truth.

'I have a proposition to put to you,' he said evenly. 'But first I need to know. Do you have a substance abuse problem, of any kind?'

'Would you believe me if I told you?'

'Yes—'

'Ri-ight.' She shook her head. 'Why are you really here?'

'I told you, I have a proposition to put to you. A business proposition.'

'It's always business, isn't it?'

Luke bit down on his irritation. Already he was regretting the insane impulse to come here. 'Enough. Either you listen to me or you don't. If you're interested in making a comeback—'

He saw her knuckles whiten around her coffee mug. 'Who said I was interested in that?'

'Why else accept the Bryant's booking?'

She raised her eyebrows. 'Boredom?'

Luke stared at her, saw the dangerous glitter in her eyes, the thin line of her mouth. The quivering chin. 'I don't think so,' he said quietly.

'Why are you interested in me making a comeback?' she challenged. 'Because you certainly weren't in New York.'

'I changed my mind.'

'Oh, really?'

'Look, I'll tell you all about it if you think we can have a civil conversation, but first just answer the question. Do you have a substance—'

'Abuse problem,' she finished wearily. 'No.'

'Have you ever?'

'No.'

'Then why were you passed out in New York?'

Her expression was blank, her voice flat. 'I hadn't eaten anything. Low blood sugar.' Luke hesitated. It hadn't seemed like just low blood sugar. She eyed him cynically. 'Clearly you believe me, just like you said you would.'

'I admit, I'm sceptical.'

'*So* honest of you.'

'I won't have anything to do with drugs.'

'That makes two of us. Amazing,' she drawled, 'we have something in common.'

He thought of the tabloids detailing her forays into rehab. The pictures of her at parties. He really should turn around and walk right out of here. Aurelie watched his face, her mouth curling into a cold smile he didn't like. 'That doesn't mean I've been a Girl Scout,' she told him. 'I never pretended I was.'

'I know that.'

'So what do you want?'

What *did* he want? The question felt loaded, the answer more complicated than he wanted it to be. 'I want you to sing. At the reopening of four of my stores.'

He felt her shock even though her expression—that cold, cynical smile—didn't change. 'Why?' she finally asked. 'You certainly didn't seem thrilled I was singing at your New York store.'

'No, I didn't,' he agreed evenly. 'Bryant Stores is important to me and I didn't particularly like the idea of endorsing a washed-up pop star as its mascot.'

'Thanks for spelling it out.'

'I've changed my mind.'

She rolled her eyes. 'Well, *that's* a relief.'

'The opening was well received—'

'Oh, yes, the papers loved the irony of a store trying to reinvent itself hiring a pop star who can't. I got that.' Bitterness spiked her words, and Luke felt a rush of something like satisfaction. She *was* trying to change.

'People still wanted to see you.'

'The most exciting part was when I almost tripped. People want to see me fail, Bryant. That's why they come.' She turned away and he gazed at her thoughtfully, saw the way the sunlight gilded the sharp angles of her profile in gold.

'I don't want to see you fail.'

'What?' She turned back to him, surprise wiping the cynicism from her face. She looked young, clear-eyed, even innocent. The truth of her revealed, and it gave him purpose. Certainty.

'I don't want to see you fail. Give yourself a second chance, Aurelie, and listen to what I have to say.'

* * *

Aurelie stared at him, wishing she hadn't revealed so much. *People want to see me fail.* Why had she told him the truth? Even if he already knew it, he hadn't known that she knew it. And, worse, that it hurt her. Yet she was pretty sure he knew now, and she hated the thought.

She hated that he was here. She couldn't act like Aurelie the go-to-hell pop princess here, in her grandma's house. Her home, the only place she'd ever been able to be herself. Be safe.

She felt a tightness in her chest, like something trying to claw its way out, finally break free. 'I want you to leave,' she said, and thankfully her voice came out flat. Strong. 'I'm not interested in anything you have to say, or any job you might have for me, so please, *please* leave.' Her voice wasn't strong then. It trembled and choked and she had to blink hard, which made her all the more furious.

Why did this man affect her like this? *So much?* In sudden, fearful moments she felt as if he saw something in her no one else did, no one else even wanted to. What a joke. There was nothing there to see. And, even if there were, he wouldn't be the one to see it. He still probably thought she did drugs.

'I will leave,' Luke said steadily. 'But please let me say something first.'

He stood in the doorway of her kitchen, so still, so sure, like a rock. A mountain. She couldn't get him out of here if she tried. Yet bizarrely—and terrifyingly—there was something steady about his presence. Something almost reassuring. Which was ridiculous because she didn't trust any men, and especially not ones who strode in and blustered and proclaimed, insisting that they were going to rescue you as if they were some stupid knight. All Luke Bryant needed was a white horse and a big sword.

Well, he *had* a big sword. She was pretty sure about that.

And she knew exactly how to knock him off his trusty steed. Men were all the same. They might say they wanted to help you or protect you, but really? They just wanted you. And Luke Bryant was no different.

'All right.' She folded her arms, gave him a cool smile. 'So tell me.'

'I'm overseeing the launch of our stores in Asia, and I'd like to hire you to perform at the reopening of each.'

'So you want me to sing *Take Me Down* at each one? Slink and shimmy and be outrageous?' The thought made her feel ill. She could not do that again. She wouldn't.

'No,' Luke said in that calm, deep voice Aurelie found bizarrely comforting. 'I don't want you to do any of those things.'

'That's what your Head of PR paid me to do.'

'And this time I'm paying you to do something else.'

She felt that creeping of suspicion, and a far more frightening flicker of hope. 'And what would that be, Mr Bossy?'

'To sing your new song. The one I heard while I was standing on your front porch.'

CHAPTER THREE

AURELIE ALMOST SWAYED, and Luke took an instinctive step towards her. Clearly he'd surprised her with that one. Well, he'd meant to. He had to do something to shock her out of that jaded superstar persona she wore like rusty armour. And the fact that he knew it was armour, no more than a mask, made him more certain.

She *was* different.

But how different? And how crazy was he, to come here and suggest they do business together? She might still possess a certain popularity, but he knew he was taking a huge risk. And he wasn't entirely sure why he was doing it.

'Well?' he asked, pushing away those irritating doubts. She had turned away from him, her arms wrapped around herself, her head slightly bowed. Luke had to fight the ridiculous and completely inappropriate impulse to put his arms around her. *That* would really go down well.

Then she lifted her head and turned to face him with an iron-hard gaze. 'You came all the way to Vermont without hearing that song, so that wasn't your original intention.'

'Actually, it was. But hearing it was a nice confirmation, I'll admit.'

She shook her head. 'How did you even know—'

'Jenna, my Head of PR, told me that you'd asked to sing a new composition.' *Some soppy folk ballad* had been her actual words, but Luke wasn't about to say that. And one glance at Aurelie's stony face told him he didn't need to.

'Somehow I don't think you came here on Jenna's recommendation,' she said flatly. 'She hated the song.'

'I'm not Jenna.'

'No,' she said, and her gaze swept over him slowly, suggestively. 'You're not.' She'd dropped her voice and it slid over him, all husky sweetness. Luke felt that prickling on the back of his neck. He hated how she affected him. Hated and needed it both at the same time, because there could be no denying the pulse of longing inside him when that husky murmur of a voice slid over him like a curtain of silk and she turned from innocent to siren. *Innocent Siren*, that had been the name of her first album.

Except there was nothing innocent about her, never had been, he was delusional to think that way—and then Luke saw she was walking towards him, her slender hips swaying, her storm cloud eyes narrowed even as a knowing smile curved those soft pink lips that looked so incredibly kissable.

'So why are you really here, Luke?' she asked softly. He felt his neurons short-circuit as, just as before, she placed one slender hand on his chest. He could feel the heat of her through the two layers of his suit, the thud of his own heart in response.

'I told you—' he began, but that was all he could get out. He could smell her perfume, that fresh, citrusy scent. And her hair tickled his lips. He definitely should have got a handle on his libido before he came here, because this woman made him *crazy*—

'I think I know why you're here,' she whispered, and then she stood up on her tiptoes and brushed her lips across his.

Sensation exploded inside him. He felt as if Catherine wheels had gone off behind his eyes, throughout his whole body. One almost-nothing kiss and he was firing up like a Roman candle.

'Don't—' he said brusquely, pulling away just a little. Not as much as he should have.

'Don't what?' she teased, her breath soft against his mouth, and then instinct and desire took over and he pulled her towards him, his mouth slanting over hers as he deepened her brush of a kiss into something primal and urgent. His arms came around her, his hands sliding down the narrow knobs of her spine to her hips where they fastened firmly as if they belonged there and he brought her against him. He claimed that little kiss, made it his.

His, not hers. Not theirs. Because in some distant part of his brain he realised she'd gone completely still, lifeless even, and all the while he was kissing her like a drowning man clinging to the last lifebelt.

With a shaming amount of effort he pushed himself away from her, let out a shuddering breath. His heart still thudded. 'What the hell was that about?'

She gazed back at him in stony-faced challenge, seeming completely unaffected by something that felt as if it had almost felled him. 'You tell me.'

'Why did you kiss me?'

'Are you trying to act like you didn't want it?'

'I—' Damn. 'No, I'm not.' Surprise rippled in her eyes like a shadow on water but she said nothing. 'I admit, I'm attracted to you. I'd rather not be. And it has nothing to do with why I came here.'

She arched her eyebrows, elegantly incredulous. 'Nothing?'

Luke expelled an exasperated breath. He didn't lie. Couldn't, ever since he'd told the truth in one of the most defining moments of his life and hadn't been believed. He'd been blamed instead, and maybe—

He pushed the thought away. 'It probably had something to do with it,' he admitted tersely. 'But I wish it didn't.'

'Really.' She sounded utterly disbelieving, and he could hardly blame her. From the first moment he'd met her his body had been reacting. Wanting. He knew it, and obviously so did she.

'Why did you kiss me?' he countered. 'Because I admit I might have taken over, but you started it and there's got to be a reason for that.'

'Does there?'

'I think,' Luke said slowly, 'there's a reason for everything you do, even if it seems completely crazy from the outside.'

She let out a little laugh, the first genuine sound of humour he'd heard from her. 'Thank you for that compliment… I think.'

'You're welcome.'

They stared at each other like two wrestlers on either side of the mat. Some kind of truce had been called, but Luke didn't know what it was. Or why he was here. His calm, no-nonsense plan to hire Aurelie for the Asia openings— to change the public's opinion of both her and the store, the ultimate reinvention—seemed like the flimsiest of pretexts after that kiss.

He'd come here because he wanted her, full stop. It really was that simple.

Aurelie stared at Luke, wondered what tack he'd try next. The honesty had surprised her. Unsettled her, because she knew he was speaking the truth and she didn't know what to do with it. She wasn't used to honesty.

Trying for something close to insouciance, she turned away from him, picked up her discarded mug of coffee and kept the kitchen counter between them.

Luke folded his arms. 'So you still haven't told me why you kissed me.'

She shrugged. 'Why not?' That kiss had started out as a way to prove he just wanted one thing and it wasn't her song. But then she'd felt the softness of his lips, his hair, and she'd forgotten she'd been trying to prove a point. She'd felt a flicker of…something. Desire? It seemed impossible. And then Luke had deepened the kiss and she'd felt herself retreat into numbness as she always did.

She took a sip of her now-cold coffee. She shouldn't have kissed him at all. She didn't want to be Aurelie here, in the only place she'd ever thought of as home. She wanted to be herself, but she didn't know how to do that with someone like Luke. Or with anyone, really. She'd been pretending for so long she wasn't sure she could stop. 'Why don't you tell me why you want to hire me for these reopenings.'

'I told you already.'

'The real reason.'

He stared at her, his dark eyes narrowed, lips thinned. He really was an attractive man, not that it mattered. Still a part of her could admire the chocolate-coloured hair, could remember how soft it had felt threaded through her fingers. How hard and toned his body had been against hers. How *warm* his eyes had seemed—

She needed to put a stop to that kind of thinking right now. 'Well? Why?'

'It's more complicated than I'd prefer it to be,' Luke said, the words seeming wrested from him. 'It makes good business sense on one level, and on another…yes.' He shrugged, spread his hands. 'Like I said before, attraction comes into it. Probably. It doesn't mean I'm going to act on it.'

'Despite the fact that you just did.'

'If you thrust your tongue into my mouth, I'll respond. I'm a man.'

Exactly. And she knew men. Still, the extent of his honesty unnerved her. He could have easily denied it. Lied. 'What are you,' she said, 'Pinocchio?'

He glanced away, his expression shuttering. 'Something like that.'

The man could not tell a lie. How fascinating, considering she told dozens. Hundreds. Her whole *life* was a lie. 'So if I asked you anything, you'd have to tell me the truth?'

'I don't like lying, if that's what you mean.'

'Don't like it, or aren't good at it?'

'Both.'

She was tempted to ask him something really revealing, embarrassing even, yet she decided not to. Any more intimacy with this man was not advisable.

'Okay, then. Tell me just what this whole Asia thing is about.'

'I'm relaunching four stores across Asia. Manila, Singapore, Hong Kong and Tokyo. I want you to sing at each opening.'

'Sing my new song.'

'That's about it.'

'That's kind of a risk, don't you think?'

He raised his eyebrows in both challenge and query. 'Is it?'

'How long were you standing on my porch?'

'Long enough.'

She had the absolutely insane impulse to ask him what he'd thought of that song. She'd been working on it for months, and it meant more to her than she ever wanted to admit—which was why she wouldn't ask. 'Why don't you want my usual Aurelie schtick?' she asked instead.

He nodded, and it felt like an affirmation. 'That's what it is, isn't it? A schtick. An act. Not who you really are.'

She didn't like the way his gaze seemed to sear right

through her. She didn't like it at all, and yet part of her was crying out yes. *Yes, it's pretend, it's not me, and you're the only person who has ever realised that.* From somewhere she dredged up the energy to roll her eyes. Laugh it off. 'Of course it's a schtick. Any famous person is just an act, Bryant. A successful one.'

'Call me Luke.' She pressed her lips together. Said nothing. He took a step towards her. 'So will you do it?'

'I can't give you an answer right now.'

'You'd better give me an answer soon, because I fly to the Philippines next week.'

She let out a low breath, shook her head. She wasn't saying no, she just felt…

'Scared?'

'What?'

'You're scared of me. Why?' She stared at him, wordless with shock, and he gave her a little toe-curling smile. 'The honesty thing? It goes both ways. I call it as I see it, Aurelie. Always. So why are you scared?'

She bristled. 'Because I don't know you. Because you practically stalked me, coming to my house here, muscling your way in—'

'I asked. Politely. And you're the one who kissed me, so—'

'Just forget it.' She turned away, hating how much he saw and didn't see at the same time. Hating how confused and needy he made her feel.

'Tell me why you're scared.'

'I'm not scared.' She was terrified.

'Are you scared of me, or of singing?' He took another step towards her, his body relaxed and so contained. He was so sure of himself, of who he was, and it made her angry. Jealous. *Scared.*

'Neither—' *Both.*

'You know you're not that great a liar, either.'

She whirled around to face him, to say something truly scathing, but unfortunately nothing came to mind. All her self-righteous indignation evaporated, and all the posturing she depended on collapsed. She had nothing. And she was so very tired of pretending, of acting as if she didn't care, of being someone else. Even if the thought of being herself— and having people see that—was utterly terrifying.

'Of course I'm a little…wary,' she snapped, unable to lose that brittle, self-protective edge. 'The press lives to ridicule me. People love to hate me. Do you think I really enjoy opening myself up to all that again and again?'

He stared at her for a moment, *saw* her, and it took all her strength to stand there and take it, not to say something stupid or suggestive, hide behind innuendo. She lifted her chin instead and returned his gaze.

'You act like you do.'

'And I told you, every famous person is an act. Aurelie the pop star isn't real.' She couldn't believe she was saying this.

'Then who,' Luke asked, 'is Aurelie Schmidt?'

Aurelie stared at him for a long, helpless moment. She had no answer to that one. She'd been famous since she was sixteen years old. 'It hardly matters. Nobody's interested in Aurelie Schmidt.'

'Maybe they would be if they got to know her.'

'Trust me, they wouldn't.'

'It's a risk you need to take.'

It was a risk too great to take. 'Don't tell me what I need.'

Luke thrust his hands into his pockets. 'Fine. Let me take you to dinner.'

Suspicion sharpened inside her. 'Why?'

'A business dinner. To discuss the details of the Asia trip.'

She started to shake her head, then stopped. Was she really

going to close this down before it had even started? Was she that much a coward? 'I haven't said yes.'

'I know.'

Slowly she let out her breath. She *was* scared. Of singing, and of him. Of how much he seemed to see. Know. And yet part of her craved it all at the same time. Desperately. 'All right.'

'Any recommendations for a good place to eat around here?'

'Not really. There's a fast food joint in the next town over—'

'Anything else?'

'Nothing closer than thirty miles.'

He said nothing, but his thoughtful gaze still unnerved her. This whole thing was a bad idea, and she should call it off right now—

'Tell you what,' Luke suggested. 'I'll cook for you.'

'What?' No man had ever cooked for her, or even offered.

'I'm not Michelin, but I make a decent steak and chips.'

'I don't have any steak.'

'Do you eat it?'

'Yes—'

'Then I'll go out and buy some. And over a meal we'll discuss Asia.'

It sounded so pleasant, so *normal*, and yet still she hesitated. Pleasant and normal were out of her realm of experience. Then she thought of what Luke was offering her—an actual *chance*—and she nodded. Grudgingly. 'Okay.'

'Good.' He turned to go. 'I'll be back in half an hour.'

Thirty minutes' respite. 'Okay,' she said again, and then he was gone.

Luke gave her nearly an hour. He thought she needed the break. Hell, he did too. He took his time choosing two thick fillets, a bag of potatoes, some salad. He thought about buying a bottle of wine, but decided against it. This was a business dinner. Strictly business, no matter how much his libido acted up or how much he remembered that mind-blowing kiss—

Hell.

He stopped right there in the drinks aisle and asked himself just what he was doing here. His brain might be insisting it was just business, but his body said otherwise. His body remembered the feel of her lips, the smoke of her voice, the emotion in her eyes. His body remembered and wanted, and that was dangerous. *Crazy.*

He straightened, forced himself to think as logically as he always did. All right, yes, he desired her. He'd admitted it. But this was still business. If Aurelie's performance at Bryant's gave her the kind of comeback he envisioned, it would create fantastic publicity for the store. It was, pure and simple, a good business move. That was why he was here.

As he resolutely turned towards the checkout, he felt a prickle of unease, even guilt. He'd told Aurelie he didn't lie, but right then he was pretty sure he was lying to himself.

By the time he made it back to the house on the end of the little town's sleepiest street it was early evening, the sun's rays just starting to mellow. The air was turning crisp, and he could see a few scarlet leaves on the maple outside the weathered clapboard house Aurelie called home.

He rang the doorbell, listened to it wheeze and then her light footsteps. She opened the door and he saw that she'd showered—squash *that* vision right now—and her hair was damp and tucked behind her ears. She'd changed into a pale green cashmere sweater and a pair of skinny jeans, and when he glanced down he saw she was wearing fuzzy pink socks. Fuchsia, actually.

He nodded towards the socks. 'Those look cosy.'

She gave him the smallest of smiles, but at least it felt real. 'My feet get cold.'

'May I come in?'

She nodded, and he sensed the lack of artifice from her. Liked it. *Who is Aurelie Schmidt?* Maybe he'd find out.

But did he really want to?

She moved aside and he came in with the bag of groceries. 'Do you mind if I make myself comfortable in your kitchen?'

She hesitated, and he could almost imagine her suggestive response. *You go ahead and make yourself comfortable anywhere, Luke.* He could practically write the script for her, because he was pretty sure now that was all it was: a script. Lines. This time she didn't give them to him; she just shrugged. 'Sure.'

He nodded and headed towards the back of the house.

Fifteen minutes later he had the steaks brushed with olive oil and in the oven, the potatoes sliced into wedges and frying on the stove, and he was tossing a salad. Aurelie perched on a stool, her fuzzy feet hooked around the rungs, and watched him.

'Do you like to cook?'

'Sometimes. I'm not a gourmet, by any means. Not like my brother Chase.'

'He's good?'

Luke shrugged. He wished he hadn't mentioned Chase, or anything to do with his family. He preferred not to dredge those dark memories up; he'd determinedly pushed them way, way down. Yet something about this woman—her fragility, perhaps—brought them swimming up again. 'He's good at most things,' he replied with a shrug. He reached for some vinaigrette. 'Do you have brothers or sisters?'

'No.' From the flat way she spoke Luke guessed she was as reluctant to talk about her family as he was to talk about his. Fine with him.

He finished tossing the salad. 'Everything should be ready in a few minutes.'

Aurelie slid off her stool to get the plates. 'It smells pretty good.'

He glanced up, smiling wryly. 'Are we actually having a civil conversation?'

'Sounds like it.' She didn't smile back, just took a deep breath, the plates held to her chest. 'Look, if you came here on some kind of mercy mission, just forget it. I don't need your pity.'

He stilled. 'I don't pity you.'

'If not pity, then what?'

A muscle bunched in his jaw. 'What are you saying?'

She lifted her chin. 'I find it hard to believe you came all the way to Vermont to ask me to sing. You hadn't even heard that song. It could have sucked. Maybe it does.'

'I admit, it was a risk.'

'So why did you come? What's the real reason?' Suspicion sharpened her voice, twisted inside him like a knife. Did she actually think he'd come here to get her into bed?

Had he?

No, damn it, this was about business. About helping the store and helping Aurelie. The ultimate reinvention. Luke laid his hands flat on the counter. 'I don't have some sexual agenda, if that's what you're thinking.'

She cocked her head. 'You're sure about that?'

He shook his head slowly. 'What kind of men have you known?'

'Lots. And they're all the same.'

'I'm different.' And he'd prove it to her. He took the plates from her, his gaze steady on her own stormy one. 'Let's eat.'

Luke dished out the meal and carried it over to the table in the alcove of the kitchen. Twilight was settling softly outside, the sky awash in violet. Used to the frantic sounds of the city, he felt the silence all around him, just like he felt Aurelie's loneliness and suspicion. 'Do you live here most of the time?' he asked.

'I do now.'

'Do you like it?'

'It'd be a pretty sad life if I didn't.'

He sat opposite her and picked up his fork and knife. 'You're not much of a one for straight answers, are you?'

She met his gaze squarely, gave a small nod of acknowledgement. 'I guess not.'

'All right. Business.' Luke forced himself to focus on the one thing he'd always focused on, and was now finding so bizarrely hard. He wanted to ask her questions about the house, her life, how she'd got to where she was. He wanted to go back in the hallway and look at the photographs on the walls, he wanted to hear her play that song, he wanted—

Business.

'It's pretty simple,' he said. 'Four engagements over a period of ten days. You sing one or two of your new songs.'

'The audience won't be expecting that.'

'I know.'

'And you're okay with that?' She raised her eyebrows. 'Because your Head of PR definitely wasn't.'

'Good thing I'm CEO of the company, then,' Luke said evenly.

'You know,' Aurelie said slowly, 'people want things to be how they expect. They want me to be what they expect. What they think I am.'

'Which is exactly why I want you to be different,' Luke countered. 'Bryant's is an institution in America and other parts of the world. So are you.'

'Now that's something I haven't been compared to before.'

'If you can change your image, then anyone can.'

'Judging by the papers, you've already changed the store's image successfully. You don't need me.'

Luke hesitated because he knew she was right, at least in part. 'I didn't like the way the press spun it,' he said after a moment.

'The whole self-deprecating thing?' she said with a twisted smile. 'Former celebrity?'

'Exactly. I want a clean sweep, home run. No backhanded compliments.'

'Maybe you should just take what you can get.'

He shook his head. 'That's not how I do business.'

She glanced away. When she spoke, her voice was low. 'What if I can't change?'

'There's only one way to find out.' Aurelie didn't say anything, but he could see her thinking about it. Wondering. Hoping, even. He decided to let her mull it over. Briskly, he continued, 'Your accommodation will be provided, and we can negotiate a new rate for the—'

'I don't care about the money.'

'I want to be fair.'

She toyed with her fork, pushing the food around on her plate. He saw she hadn't eaten much. 'This still feels like pity.'

'It isn't.'

She glanced up and he saw the ghost of a smile on her face, like a remnant of who she had once been, a whisper of who she could be, if she smiled more. If she were happy. 'And you can't tell a lie, can you?'

'I won't tell a lie.'

She eyed him narrowly. 'But it's something close to pity.'

'Sympathy, perhaps.'

'Which is just a nicer word for pity.'

'Semantics.'

'Exactly.'

His lips twitched in a smile of his own. 'Okay, look. I told you, I don't pity you. I feel—'

'Sorry for me.'

'Stop putting words in my mouth. I feel…' He let out a whoosh of exasperated breath. He didn't like talking about feelings. He never did. His mother had died when he was thirteen, his father had never got close, and his brothers didn't ask. But here he was, and she was right, he couldn't lie. Not to her. 'I know how you feel,' he said at last, and she raised her eyebrows, clearly surprised by that admission. Hell, he was surprised too.

'How so?'

'I know what it feels like to want to change.'

'You've wanted to change?'

'Hasn't everybody?'

'That's no answer.'

He shrugged. 'I've had my own obstacles to overcome.'

'Like what?'

He should never have started this. The last thing he wanted to do was rake up his own tortured memories. 'A difficult childhood.'

Her mouth pursed. 'Poor little rich boy?'

He tensed, and then forced himself to relax. 'Something like that.'

She lifted her chin, challenge sparking in her eyes. 'Well, maybe I don't want to change.'

It was such obvious bravado that Luke almost laughed. 'Then why write a different kind of song? Why ask to sing it? Why accept the Bryant's booking when you haven't performed publicly in years?'

Her mouth twisted. 'Done a little Internet stalking, have you?'

'I didn't need to look on the Internet to know that.' She shook her head, said nothing. 'Anyway,' he continued in a brisker voice, 'the point is, I've been trying to reinvent Bryant's for years and—'

'What's been stopping you?'

Luke hesitated. He didn't want to bring up Aaron and his constant quest for control. 'Change doesn't happen overnight,' he finally said. 'And Bryant's has a century-old reputation. There's been resistance.'

'There always is.'

'So see? We have something else in common.'

'You want to reinvent a store and I want to reinvent myself.'

Luke didn't answer, because there was an edge to her voice that made him think a simple agreement was not the right choice here. He waited, wondered why it mattered to him so much.

He didn't need Aurelie. He didn't need her to open a store or sing a damn song. He didn't need her at all.

Yet as she gazed at him with those rain-washed eyes he felt a tug deep inside that he couldn't begin to understand. More than lust, deeper than need. Despite having had three long-term satisfying relationships, he'd never felt this whirlpool of emotion before, as if he were being dragged under by the force of his own feelings. Never mind her being scared. He was terrified.

The smart thing to do right now would be to get out of this chair, out of this house. Walk away from Aurelie and all her crazy complications and go about his business, his *life*, the way he always had. Calm and in control, getting things done, never going too deep.

He didn't move.

Aurelie drew a deep breath, let it out slowly. 'Let me play you my song,' she finally said and, surprised and even touched, Luke nodded.

'I'd like that.'

She smiled faintly, that whisper of a promise, and word-lessly Luke followed her out of the room.

CHAPTER FOUR

AURELIE LED LUKE into the music room at the front of the house, her heart thudding, her skin turning clammy. She felt dizzy with nerves, and silently prayed that she wouldn't pass out. The last thing she needed was Luke Bryant to think she'd ODed again.

She paused in front of the piano, half-regretting her suggestion already. No, not even half—*totally*. Why was she opening herself up to this? She didn't need money. She didn't need to sing in public again. She didn't need any of this.

But she wanted it. She actually wanted to share something that was important to her, share it with this man, never mind the public, even as it scared her near witless.

'Aurelie?'

There was something about the way he said her name, so quietly, so *gently*, that made her ache deep inside. She swallowed, her face turned away from him. 'It sounds better with guitar.'

'Okay.'

She reached for her acoustic guitar, the one her grandmother had bought her just before she'd died. *Don't forget who you really are, Aurie. Don't let them turn your head.* But she had let them. She'd forgotten completely. Her fingers curled around the neck of the guitar and, unable to look at Luke—afraid to see the expression on his face—she bent her head and busied herself with tuning the instrument. Need-lessly, since she'd played it that afternoon.

After a few taut minutes she knew she couldn't wait any longer. Yet she was terrified to play the song, terrified to have Luke reject it. *Her.* He'd let her down easily because, no matter what he said, she knew he did feel sorry for her. But it would still hurt.

'So has this song got some kind of long silent intro or what?'

She let out a little huff of laughter, glad he'd jolted her out of her ridiculous stage fright. 'Patience.' And taking a deep breath, she began. The first few melancholy chords seemed to flow through her, out into the room. And then she began to sing, not one of the belt-it-out numbers of her pop star days, but something low and intimate and tender. *'Winter came so early, it caught me by surprise. I stand alone till the cold wind blows the tears into my eyes.'* She hesitated for a tiny second, trying to gauge Luke's reaction, but the song seemed to take up all the space. *'I turn my face into the wind and listen to the sound. Never give your heart away. It will only bring you down.'* And then she forgot about Luke, and just sang. The song took over everything.

Yet when the last chord died away and the room seemed to bristle with silence, she felt her heart thud again and she couldn't look at him. Staring down at her guitar, she idly picked a few strings. 'It's kind of a downer of a song, isn't it?' she said with an unsteady little laugh. 'Probably not the best number to open a store with.'

'That doesn't matter.' She couldn't tell a thing from his tone, and she still couldn't look at him. 'Of course, if you had another one, maybe a *bit* more hopeful, you could sing that one too.'

Something leapt inside her, a mongrel beast of hope and fear. A dangerous animal. She looked up, saw him gazing at her steadily, yet without any expression she could define. 'I could?'

'Yes.'

'So...' She swallowed. 'What did you think? Of the song?'

'I thought,' Luke said quietly, with obvious and utter sincerity, 'it was amazing.'

'Oh.' She looked back down at her guitar, felt tears sting her eyes and blinked hard to keep them back. Damn it, she was not going to cry in front of this man. Not now. Not ever. 'Well...good.' She kept her head lowered, and then she felt Luke shift. He'd been sitting across from her, but now he leaned forward, his knee almost nudging hers.

'I can understand why you're scared.'

Instinct kicked in. 'I never actually said I was scared.' And then she sniffed, loudly, which basically blew her cover.

'You didn't have to.' He placed one hand on her knee, and she gazed down at it, large, brown, strong. Comforting. 'That song is very personal.'

Which was why she felt so...*naked* right now, every protective layer peeled away. She swallowed, stared at his hand, mesmerised by the long, lean fingers curled unconsciously around her knee. 'It's just a song.'

'Is it?'

And then she looked up at him, and knew she was in trouble. He was gazing at her with such gentle understanding, such tender compassion, that she felt completely exposed and accepted at the same time. It was such a weird feeling, such an *overwhelming* feeling, that it was almost painful. She swallowed. 'Luke...' Her voice came out husky, and she saw his pupils flare. Felt the very air tauten. This tender moment was turning into something else, something Aurelie knew and understood.

This was about sex. It was always about sex. And while part of her felt disappointed, another part flared to life.

Luke straightened, taking his hand from her knee. 'I should go. It's late.'

'You can't drive all the way back to New York tonight.'

'I'll find a place to stay.' He made to rise from his chair, and Aurelie felt panic flutter like a trapped, desperate bird inside her.

'You could stay here.'

He stared at her, expressionless, and Aurelie put away her guitar, her face averted from his narrowed gaze. Her heart was pounding again. She didn't know what she was telling him. What she wanted. All she knew was she didn't want him to go.

'I don't think that's a good idea,' Luke said after a moment and Aurelie turned to face him.

'Why not?'

He smiled wryly, but she saw how dark and shadowed his eyes looked. 'Because we're going to have a business relationship and I don't want to complicate things.'

She lifted her eyebrows, tried for insouciance. 'Why does it have to be complicated?'

'What are you asking me, Aurelie?'

She liked the way he said her name. She'd always hated it, a ridiculous name given to her by an even more ridiculous mother, but when he said it she felt different. She felt more like herself—or at least the person she thought she could be, if given a chance. 'What do you want me to be asking you?'

He laughed softly. 'Never a straight answer.'

'I'd hate to bore you.'

'I don't think you could ever bore me.' He was staring straight at her, and she could see the heat in his eyes. Felt it in herself, a flaring deep within, which was sudden and surprising because desire for a man was something she hadn't felt in a long time, if ever. Yet she felt it now, for this man. This wasn't about power or control or the barter that sex had always been to her. She simply wanted him, wanted to be with him.

'Well?' she asked, her voice no more than a breath.

Luke didn't move. Didn't speak. Aurelie saw both the doubt and desire in his eyes, and she took a step towards him so she was standing between his splayed thighs. With her fingertips she smoothed the crease that had appeared in his forehead. 'You think too much.'

His mouth curved wryly. 'I think I'm thinking with the wrong organ at the moment.'

She laughed softly. 'What's wrong with thinking with that organ on occasion?' She let her fingertips drift from his forehead to his cheek, felt the bristle of stubble on his jaw. She liked touching him. How strange. How *nice*.

Luke closed his eyes. 'I really don't think this is a good idea.'

'That's your brain talking now.'

'Yes—'

She let her thumb rest on his lips. They were soft and full and yet incredibly masculine. With his eyes closed she had the freedom to study his face, admire the strong lines of his jaw and nose, the sooty sweep of his lashes. Long lashes and full lips on such a virile man. Amazing.

'Shh,' she said softly, and then slowly, deliberately, she slid her finger into his mouth. His lips parted, and she felt the wet warmth of his tongue before he bit softly on the pad of her finger. Lust jolted like an electric pulse low in her belly, shocking her. Thrilling her. Luke opened his eyes; they blazed with heat and need. He sucked gently on her finger and she let out a shuddery little gasp.

Then he drew back, his eyes narrowing once more. 'Why are you doing this?'

She smiled. 'Why not?'

'I don't want you throwing this in my face, telling me I'm just like every other man you've met.'

'I won't.' She knew he wasn't. He was different, just like he'd said he was. And she wanted him to stay. She *needed* him to stay. 'You really do think too much,' she murmured. She stepped closer, hooked one leg around his. She hooked her other leg around so she was straddling him. Then she lowered herself, legs locked around his, onto his lap. She could feel his arousal pressing against her and she shifted closer, settling herself against him.

'That's a rather graceful move,' Luke said, the words coming out on a half-groan.

'All that dancing onstage has made me *very* flexible.'

'Aurelie…'

'I like how you say my name.'

Luke slid his hands down her back, anchored onto her hips, holding her there. 'This really isn't a good idea,' he muttered, and Aurelie pressed against him.

'Define good,' she said, and as he drew her even closer she knew she had him. She'd won, and she felt a surge of both triumph and desire. Yet amidst that welter of emotion she felt a little needle of disappointment, of hurt. Men really were all the same.

He was being seduced. Luke had realised this at least fifteen minutes ago, when Aurelie had first got that knowing glint in her eyes, and even though just about everything in him was telling him this was a bad idea, his body was saying something else entirely. His body was shouting, *Hell, yes.*

He felt as if he were two men, one who stood about five feet behind him, coldly rational, pointing out that he was doing exactly what Aurelie had accused him of doing. Coming here with a sexual agenda, with a plan to get her into bed—

Except she was the one trying to get *him* into bed.

And he wanted to go there.

Still, that cold voice pointed out, sleeping with Aurelie was a huge mistake, one that would cause countless complications for their proposed business trip to Asia, not to mention his personal life. His *sanity.*

The other man, the one curving his hands around her hips, was insisting that he wasn't sleeping with Aurelie, he was sleeping with Aurelie *Schmidt.* The woman who had sung that beautiful, heartbreaking song, who hid her heart in her eyes, whom he'd recognised from the first moment she'd looked up at him.

Yet maybe that was even worse. That woman was confusing, vulnerable, and far more desirable than any persona she put on. And whether it was the pop star or the hidden woman underneath on his lap, he knew it was still a hell of a mistake.

And one he had decided to make. Luke slid his hands up her back to cradle her face, his fingers threading through the softness of her hair. And then he kissed her, his lips brushing once, twice over hers before he let himself go deep and the coldly rational part of himself telling him to stop went silent.

Somehow they got upstairs. It was hazy in his mind, fogged as it was with lust, but Luke remembered stumbling on a creaky stair, opening a door. There was a bed, wide and rumpled. And there was Aurelie, standing in front of it, a faint smile on her face. Luke slid her sweater over her head, unbuttoned her jeans. She wriggled out of them and lay on the bed in just her bra and underwear, waiting, ready.

Except her damn chin was quivering.

Luke hesitated, the roar of his heated blood and his own aching need almost, almost winning out. 'Aurelie—'

He saw uncertainty flicker in her eyes, shadows on water, and then she reached up to grab him by the lapels of his suit; he was still completely dressed.

'It's too late for second thoughts,' she said, and as she

kissed him, a hungry, open-mouthed kiss, he had to agree that it just might be.

He kissed her back, desire for her surging over him in a tidal wave, drowning out anything but that all-consuming need, and he felt her fumble with the zip of his trousers.

'Aurelie...' He groaned her name, felt her fingers slide around him. He pushed aside the lacy scrap of her underwear, stroked the silkiness of her thigh. He slid his fingers higher, kissed her deeper, his body pulsing with need, aching with want. Yet even as his hands roamed over her, teasing and finding, a part of his brain started to buzz.

Distantly he realised she'd stopped responding. Her arms had fallen away from him and she was lying tensely beneath him, stiff and straight.

She let out a shudder that could have been a sob or a sigh, and Luke pulled back to look down at her.

Her eyes were scrunched shut, her breathing ragged, her whole body radiating tension. She looked, he thought with a savage twist of self-loathing, as if she were being tortured.

Swearing, Luke rolled off her. His body ached with unfulfilment and his mind seethed with regret. He'd *known* this was a mistake.

He raked a hand through his sweat-dampened hair, let out a shuddering breath. 'What happened?' he asked in a low voice, but Aurelie didn't answer. Silently she slid off the bed and disappeared into the bathroom. Luke heard the door shut and he threw an arm over his eyes. He didn't know what had just happened, but he was pretty sure it was his fault.

From behind the closed door he heard her moving around, a cupboard opening and closing. Seconds ticked by, then minutes. Unease crawled through him, mingling with the virulent regret and even shame he felt. He hated locked doors. Hated that damning silence, the helplessness he felt on the other side, the creeping sense that something wasn't right. Something was very, very wrong.

He got up from the bed, pulled up his trousers and buckled his belt, then headed over to the door.

'Aurelie?' No answer. His unease intensified. 'Aurelie,' he said again and opened the door.

As soon as he saw her Luke swore.

She stood in front of the sink, one arm outstretched, a fully loaded syringe in the other. Acting only on instinct, Luke knocked the syringe hard out of her hand and it went clattering to the floor.

Aurelie stilled, her face expressionless. 'Well, *that* was a waste,' she finally said, her voice a drawl, and bent to pick up the syringe.

'What the hell are you doing?'

She eyed him sardonically. 'I think the more important question is, what do you think I'm doing?'

He stared at her, confusion, fury and shame all rushing through him in a scalding river. This woman drove him *insane*.

Would you believe me if I told you I didn't? He'd said he would. 'It looks,' he said as evenly as he could, 'like you're shooting yourself up with some kind of drug.'

Her lips curved in that way he knew and hated. Mockery. Armour. 'You get a gold star,' she said as she swabbed off the syringe with a cotton pad and some rubbing alcohol. 'That's exactly what I'm doing.'

And he watched as she carefully injected the syringe into the fleshy part of her upper arm.

Luke felt his hands clench into fists at his sides. 'Why don't you tell me what's really going on here?'

She put the syringe away in a little black cosmetic bag. Luke glimpsed a few clear phials inside before she zipped it up and put it away. She gave a small, tired sigh. 'Don't worry, Bryant. It's only insulin.'

She walked past him back into the bedroom, and Luke turned around to stare at her. '*Insulin?* You have diabetes?'

'Bingo.' She reached for a fuzzy bathrobe hanging on the back of the door and put it on. Sitting on the edge of the bed, swallowed up by fleece, she looked young and vulnerable and so very alone.

'Why didn't you tell me?'

'When should I have done that? When I was passed out on the dressing room floor, or after you dunked me in the sink?'

Slowly he walked into the bedroom, sank onto a chair across from her. He raked his hands through his hair, tried to untangle his tortured, twisted thoughts. 'So when you were passed out in New York, it was because of low blood sugar?' Just like she'd said.

'I forgot to check my bloods before I went.'

'That's dangerous—'

She let out a short laugh. 'Thanks for the warning. Trust me, I know. I've been living with diabetes for almost ten years. I was keyed up about the performance and I forgot.' And then as if she realised she'd revealed too much, she folded her arms and looked away, jaw set, eyes hard.

'Why didn't you tell me earlier? In the kitchen, when I *asked*?'

'You wouldn't have believed me—'

'I said I would—'

'Oh, yes, you *said*.' Her eyes flashed malice. 'Well, maybe you're not such a Boy Scout after all, because I don't think you were telling the truth.'

'It was,' Luke said, an edge creeping into his voice, 'a little hard to believe you were passed out just from lack of food. If I'd known you had a *condition*—'

'And maybe I don't feel like explaining myself every time

something looks a little suspicious,' she snapped. 'If you were passed out, would someone assume you'd done drugs? Were a junkie?'

'No, of course not. But I'm not—'

She leaned forward, eyes glittering. 'You're not what?'

Luke stared at her, his mind still spinning. 'I'm not you,' he said at last. 'You're *Aurelie.*' The moment he said it, he knew it had been completely the wrong thing to say. To think.

She turned away from him, her jaw set. 'I am, aren't I,' she said quietly.

Luke dropped his head in his hands. 'I only meant you've been known to…to…'

'I know what I've been known to do.' Her eyes flashed, her chin trembled. He could always tell the truth of her from that chin. She was scared. And sad. Hell, so was he. *How had they got here?*

He shook his head, weary and heartsick, but also angry. 'What happened back there on the bed, Aurelie? Why did you look like…' He could barely say it. 'Like you were being tortured? Or attacked? Were you trying to prove some point?' Had she set him up, shown him to be exactly what she'd accused, just another man determined to get her into bed? 'Well, I guess you made it,' he said heavily when she didn't answer. 'Congratulations.'

Still she said nothing, just stared him down, and in that silence Luke wondered if things could have turned out any worse.

'Do you still want me to go?' she finally asked. 'To Asia?'

He let out a short, disbelieving laugh. 'Do you still *want* to go? After this?'

She raised her eyebrows, her expression so very cold. 'Why shouldn't I?'

He felt a rush of anger, cleaner than shame. She'd *played* him. Admittedly, he'd let himself be played. He'd been willing to be seduced, had turned it to his advantage. But the fact remained that she'd used him, coldly and deliberately, to prove some twisted, paranoid point. He hadn't had a sexual agenda until she'd sat in his lap.

Liar.

'Yes, you can go to Asia,' he told her wearily. Something good would come out of this unholy affair. 'I'll have my PA email you the details. You need to be in Manila on the twenty-fourth.' With that he stood up and he saw, with some gratification, that her eyes had widened.

'You're going?'

'I don't want to stay and, frankly, I don't think you want me to, either. Like I said, you made your point.'

She stared at him, still swallowed up by her bathrobe, her eyes wide and stormy. Luke felt the shame slither inside him again. 'I didn't come here intending to sleep with you,' he said. 'I swear to God I didn't.'

She said nothing and with a shake of his head he left the room.

CHAPTER FIVE

AURELIE GAZED AT her reflection for the fifth time in the hall mirror of the deluxe suite Luke had booked for her in the Mandarin Oriental in Manila's business district. She'd arrived a few hours ago and was meeting Luke in the bar in ten minutes.

And she was sick and dizzy with nerves.

She let out a deep breath and checked her reflection again. She wore just basic make-up, mostly to disguise the violet circles under her eyes since she hadn't had a decent night's sleep since Luke had walked out of her bedroom ten days ago.

She closed her eyes briefly, the memories making her even dizzier. She couldn't think about Luke without reliving that awful encounter. The condemnation and disgust in his eyes. The *confusion*. And her own impossible behaviour.

She hadn't brought him to her bed to set him up, the way Luke had so obviously thought. She'd been acting out of need and maybe even desire—at least at first. When she'd touched him she'd felt something unfurl inside her, something that had been desperately seeking light. But then it had all gone wrong, as it always did. The moment she was stretched out on that bed she'd gone numb. He'd become just a man who wanted something from her, and he'd get it, no matter what. She'd give it to him, because that was what she did.

Except he hadn't taken it, which made him different from every other man she'd known. Why did that thought scare her so much?

He obviously didn't think *she* was different. She could still see the look of disgust twisting Luke's features, the condemnation in his eyes when he'd opened the door to the bathroom. He thought she'd been doing drugs. And then those damning words, words she felt were engraved on her heart, tattooed on her forehead. Impossible to escape.

You're Aurelie.

For a little while she'd thought he believed she wasn't but now she knew the truth. He might want her to be different on stage, but he didn't think she could really change as a person.

Aurelie with a folk ballad and guitar was just another act to Luke Bryant, a successful one that would help with his stupid store openings.

And as long as she remembered that, she'd be fine. No more longing to reach or be reached. To know or be known. No more giving in to that fragile need, that fledgling desire.

This was business, strictly business, a chance for her to validate her career if not her very self. And that was fine. She'd make sure it was.

Aurelie straightened, briskly checked her reflection for the sixth time. She looked a little pale, a bit drawn, but overall okay. The lime-green shift dress struck, she hoped, the right note between fun and professional. With a deep breath, she left her suite and went downstairs to meet Luke.

The tropical heat of the Philippines had hit her the moment she'd stepped off the plane, and she felt it drape over her once more as she stepped outside like a hot, wet blanket. Luke had texted her to say he'd meet her in the patio bar and she walked through the velvety darkness looking for him, the palm trees rustling in a sultry breeze, the sounds of a vibrant and never-sleeping city carrying on the humid air.

She found him sitting on a stool by the bar, and everything inside her seemed to lurch as she looked at him. He wore a slightly rumpled suit, his tie loosened, and in the glint of the bar's dim lighting she could see the shadow of stubble on his jaw. His head was bowed and he held a half-drunk tumbler of whisky in his hand. She stared at him almost as she would a stranger, for he looked so different and yet so much the same. So *sexy*.

Then he glanced up and as he caught sight of her it was as if that sexy stranger had been replaced by a mannequin. His face went blank, his eyes veiled even as his lips curved in a meaningless smile and he crossed the patio towards her.

'Aurelie.' He kept his gaze firmly on her face, that cool, professional smile in place. He didn't offer her a hand to shake or touch her in any way. Stupidly, she felt his chilly withdrawal like a personal rejection.

No, she would not let this be personal. This was her chance at a comeback, and to hell with Luke Bryant.

'Luke.' She nodded back at him, tried to ignore the painful pounding of her heart. *This didn't hurt.*

'Would you like a drink?'

'Just sparkling water, please.'

Luke signalled to the bartender and ushered her towards a private table tucked in the corner, shaded by a palm tree.

'Trip all right?' he asked briskly. 'Your suite?'

'Everything's lovely.'

'Good.'

The bartender came with their drinks and Aurelie sipped hers gratefully. She had no idea what to say to this man. She didn't *know* this man. And she knew that shouldn't be a surprise.

'So everything is set for tomorrow,' he said, still all brisk business. 'I have a staff person on site, Lia, who will tour you around the store, get you sorted for the performance at three.'

Aurelie stared at his blank eyes and brisk smile and thought suddenly, *You're lying.* So much for honesty. This whole conversation was forced, fake. A lie.

Yet she had no idea what he really felt. Was he disgusted with her, with who he thought she was? *You're Aurelie.*

Or could she dare hope that some remnant remained of the man who had smiled at her with such compassion, such understanding, and seemed to believe she was different?

No, she didn't dare. There was no point.

'That all sounds fine,' she said, and he nodded.

'Good.' He hadn't finished his drink, but he pushed it away from him, clearly done. 'I'm afraid I have quite a lot of work to do, but I'll probably see you at the opening.'

Probably? Aurelie felt her throat go tight and took another sip of water. Somehow she managed a breezy smile. 'That sounds fine,' she said again, knowing she was being inane, but then he was too. This whole conversation was ridiculous. And a desperate part of her still craved something real.

'Fine,' Luke said, and with one more nod he rose from the chair. Aurelie rose too. She hadn't finished her water but neither was she about to sit in the bar alone. So that was it. Yet what had she really expected?

Even so, she could not keep a sense of desolation from sweeping emptily through her as Luke strode away from the bar without a backward glance.

That went well. *Not.* Luke tugged his tie from his collar and blew out his breath. He knew he didn't possess the charm of his brother Chase or Aaron's unending arrogance, but he could definitely have handled that conversation better. He'd been trying to keep it brisk and professional, but every time he looked at her he remembered how she'd felt in his arms, how much emotion and desire she'd stirred up in him, and business went right out of the window.

Maybe it wasn't actually Aurelie who was doing this to him. Maybe he was just out of practice. He hadn't had sex in a while, and he'd always been careful with his partners. A relationship came first with him, always had, because he'd never wanted to be like his father, going after everything in a skirt and ruining his mother's life in the process.

But maybe if he'd indulged in a few more flings, he wouldn't be feeling so…lost now. He'd gone over their encounter—was there really another word for it?—far too many times in his mind. Wondered when it had started to go wrong, and why. Had Aurelie been setting him up, the way he'd believed? Proving her damn point that he'd only come there to get into her bed? It seemed obvious, and yet a gut-deep instinct told him it wasn't the whole story.

He remembered the raw ache in her voice when she'd spoken to him. *I like how you say my name.* The way her fingers had trailed down his cheek, eager and hesitant at the same time, the tremble of her slender body against his. She'd felt something then. Something real.

And then she'd gone so horribly still beneath him and he'd felt as if he were…*attacking* her. He'd never felt so repulsed, so ashamed.

The best thing to do, he told himself now, the *only* thing to do, was to avoid her. Easier for both of them. He'd only suggested this meeting as a way to clear the air, draw a firm line under what had happened. And that at least had been accomplished, even if he still felt far from satisfied in any way.

As he headed back up to his suite, Luke had a feeling the next ten days were going to be a whole new kind of hell.

Aurelie stood to the side of the makeshift stage in Bryant's lobby and tried not to hyperventilate. A thousand people mingled in the soaring space, all modern chrome and glass, so different from the historic and genteel feeling of the New York store.

She'd spent the morning with Lia, touring all ten floors of the store on Ayala Avenue and then running through sound checks and getting ready. And trying not to think about what lay ahead.

What was happening *now*, with the crowd waiting for her to walk out and be Aurelie.

Fear washed coldly through her, made her dizzy. At least she'd checked her blood sugar. If she passed out now, it would simply be from nerves.

'Thirty seconds.' The guy who was doing the sound nodded towards her, and somehow Aurelie nodded back. She was miked, ready to go—and terrified.

She peeped out at the audience, saw the excited crowd, some of them clutching posters or CDs for her to sign. They were, she knew, expecting her to prance out there and sing *Take Me Down* or one of the other boppy, salacious numbers that had made her famous. They wanted her to sing and shimmy and be outrageous, and she was going to come out in her jeans, holding her guitar, and give everyone an almighty shock.

What had she been thinking, agreeing to this? What had Luke been thinking, suggesting it? It wasn't going to work. It was all going to go hideously, horribly wrong, for the store, for her, for everyone, and it was too late to do anything about it.

She closed her eyes, terror racing through her.

I can't do this. I can't change.

She wished, suddenly and desperately, that Luke were here. A totally stupid thing to want considering how cold he'd been to her last night, but just the memory of his voice, his tender, gentle look when he'd said her song was amazing gave her a little surge of both longing and courage.

'You're on.'

On wobbly, jelly-like legs she walked onto the stage. Considering she'd played sold-out concerts in the biggest arenas in the world, she should not be feeling nervous. At all. This was a tiny stage, a tiny audience. This was nothing.

And yet it was everything.

She felt the ripple of uneasy surprise go through the audience at the sight of her, felt it like a serpent slithering round the room, ready to strike. Already she was not what anybody had expected.

She sat on the stool in the centre of the stage, hooked her feet around the rungs and looked up to stare straight at Luke. He stood at the back of the lobby near the doors, but it was a small enough space she could make out his expression completely.

He looked cold, hard and completely unyielding. Their gazes met and, his mouth thinning, he looked away. Aurelie tensed, felt herself go brittle, shiny.

'Give us a song,' someone called out, impatience audible. 'Give us Aurelie!'

Well, that was easy enough. That was who she was. Drawing a deep breath, she started to play.

Luke stood in the back of the lobby waiting for Aurelie to come on, battling a disagreeable mix of anxiety and impatience. He'd been deliberately avoiding her since their drink together last night, had convinced himself that it was the best way forward. Yet, standing there alone, he felt an irritating needle of doubt prick his conscience.

Avoidance had never been his style. Avoidance meant letting someone down, and that was something he never intended to do again. He'd worked hard all his adult life to exorcise the ghosts of his past, to earn the trust and respect of those around him.

Even Aurelie's.

He didn't like the thought of her getting ready for this performance on her own. He knew this had to be pretty terrifying for her. He should have sought her out, offered her—what? Some encouragement?

He knew where that led.

No, it was better this way. It had to be. And it wasn't as if Aurelie actually needed him.

Luke heard the ripple of uneasy surprise move through the audience as she walked onto the stage. She looked vibrant and beautiful in a beaded top and jeans, her hair loose about her shoulders. Then she looked at him, her eyes so wide and clear, and a sudden, sharp longing pierced him. He looked away.

Someone called out, and Aurelie started to play. It took him a few stunned seconds to realise she wasn't singing the song he'd heard in her house back in Vermont. She was singing one of her old hits, the same boppy number she'd sung in New York, but this time to acoustic guitar. She glanced up from her guitar, gave the audience a knowing, dirty smile. A classic Aurelie look, and one Luke already hated. Everyone cheered.

Disappointment and frustration blazed through him. This wasn't what they'd agreed. Why had she changed their deal? Was it fear—or some kind of twisted revenge?

The song ended, and Luke heard the familiar mixture of catcalls and cheers. Nothing had changed. So much for the ultimate reinvention. Aurelie walked off the stage, and even though there were several local dignitaries waiting for him to escort them through the store, Luke turned and walked away from it all.

He found her in the break room she'd been using, just as before, to change. Her back was to him as she put her guitar away, and under the flowing top he could see the knobs of her spine, the bared nape of her neck as she bent her head. Desire and anger flared inside him, one giving life to the other.

'You didn't play your song.'

She turned towards him, her face completely expressionless. 'Actually, I did.'

'You know what I mean.'

'It wasn't going to work. I warned you, you know.'

'You didn't give it a chance.'

'I could tell. Honestly, Bryant, you should be thanking me. I just saved your ass.'

'You saved your own,' he retorted. 'What happened, you chickened out?'

'I prefer to think of it as being realistic.'

Frustration bit at him. 'I didn't hire you to be Aurelie all over again.'

'Oh?' She raised her eyebrows, her mouth curving in that familiar, cynical smile, innuendo heavy in her tone. 'What *did* you hire me for?'

He shook his head, the movement violent. 'Don't.'

'Don't what?'

'Don't,' Luke ground out, 'make this about sex.'

'Everything's about sex.'

'For you, maybe.'

'Oh, and not for you? Not for the saintly Luke Bryant who said he had a business proposition for me and two hours later was in my bed?'

Luke felt his fists clench. 'You wanted me there.' At least at the start.

'I've never denied it. You're the one swimming down that river.'

His nails bit into his palms. This woman made him feel so *much*. 'I'm not denying anything. I never have.' He let out a long, low breath, forced himself to unclench his fists.

To think—and react—calmly. 'Look, we obviously need to talk. I have to go out there again, see people—'

'Do your schtick?' She gave him the ghost of a smile, and Luke smiled back.

'Yeah. I guess everyone has one.' For one bittersweet moment he felt they were in agreement, they understood each other. Then Aurelie looked away, her expression veiled once more, and Luke felt the familiar weary frustration rush through him. 'But we are going to talk,' he told her. 'There are things I have to say.' She just shrugged, and with a sigh Luke turned towards the door.

Aurelie let out a shuddering breath as she heard the door close behind him. She put her hands up to her face, felt her whole body tremble. *Why* had she done that? Acted like Aurelie, not just to a faceless audience, but to *him*?

She'd been reacting again, she knew, to the rejection. It didn't take a rocket scientist to figure that out. Nobody would let her change, so she wouldn't. It was, she knew, a pretty pathetic way of trying to stay in control.

And clearly it wasn't working because she didn't feel remotely in control. She felt as if she were teetering on the edge of an abyss, about to fall, and she didn't know what waited darkly beneath her.

Maybe this whole thing had been a mistake. Trying to change. Wanting to be different. The audiences weren't going to accept it. *Her.* And, no matter how he fussed and fumed, neither was Luke.

Drawing another deep breath, Aurelie reached for her bag. She'd fix her make-up, and then she'd go out and mingle. Smile and chat. She'd get through this day and then she'd tell Luke she was going home. She was done.

* * *

Four hours later the opening was over and Aurelie was back in her suite at the Mandarin, exhausted and heartsore. She'd managed to avoid Luke for the entire afternoon, although she'd been aware of him. Even as she chatted and smiled and laughed, nodded sympathetically when people told her they didn't really like the guitar or the jeans, she'd been watching him. *Feeling* him.

He looked so serious when he talked to people. He frowned too much. He stood stiffly, almost to attention. Yet, despite all of it, Aurelie knew he was being himself. Being real.

Something she was too afraid to be.

She'd been resigned to giving up the rest of the tour and going back to Vermont. Staying safe. Being a coward. Yet four hours later Aurelie resisted the thought of slinking away like a scolded child. Never mind what Luke thought, what anyone in the audience thought or even wanted. She needed to do this for herself.

Yet the realisation filled her only with an endless ache of exhaustion. She didn't think she had the strength to go on acting as if she didn't care when she did, so very much.

Wearily she kicked off her heels and stripped the clothes from her body. She needed a stingingly hot shower to wipe away all the traces of today. She knew Luke had said he wanted to talk to her, but the last time she'd seen him he'd been in deep discussion with several official-looking types. He'd probably forgotten all about her and the things he supposedly needed to say.

Fifteen minutes later, just as she'd slipped into a T-shirt and worn yoga pants, a knock sounded on the door. Aurelie sucked in a deep breath and ran her fingers through her hair, still damp from her shower. A peep through the eyehole confirmed her suspicions. Luke hadn't forgotten about her after all.

She opened the door and something inside her tugged hard at the sight of him, his hair a little mussed, his suit a little rumpled. He looked tired.

'Long day?' she asked and he nodded tersely.

'You could say that. May I come in?'

He always asked, she thought. Always asked her permission. Strangely, stupidly, it touched her. 'Okay.'

She stepped aside and Luke came into the sitting area of the suite. She saw his glance flick to the bedroom, visible through an open door, the wide bed piled high with silken pillows.

Then he turned back to face her with a grim, iron-hard resolution. 'We need to talk.'

With a shrug she spread her hands wide and moved to sit on the sofa, as though she were actually relaxed. 'Then talk.'

He let out a long, low breath. 'I'm sorry about the way things happened back in Vermont. I didn't want it to be like that between us.'

He looked so intent, so sincere, that mockery felt like her only defence. '*Us*, Bryant?'

'Don't call me Bryant. My name is Luke and, considering we almost slept together, I think you can manage my first name.'

She tensed. 'Almost being the key word. That doesn't give you some kind of right—'

'I'm not talking about rights, just common civility.' He sat across from her, his hands on his thighs, his face still grim. 'I'm being honest here, Aurelie—'

'Sorry,' she drawled, 'that doesn't score any Brownie points. I already know you can't be anything else.'

'Just stop it,' he bit out. 'Stop it with the snappy one-liners and the bored tone and world-weary cynicism—'

'My, that's *quite* a list—'

'Stop.' He leaned forward, his face twisting with frustration or maybe even anger. 'Stop being so damn fake.'

She stilled. Said nothing, because suddenly she had nothing to say. She'd defaulted to her Aurelie persona, to the bored indifference she used as a shield, but Luke saw through it all. He stared at her now, those dark eyes blazing, burning right through her. She swallowed and looked down at her lap. 'What do you want from me?' she asked in a low voice.

'I want to know what *you* want from *me.*'

She looked up, surprise rendering her speechless once more. Her throat dry, she forced herself to shrug. 'I don't want anything from you.'

'Why did you want to sleep with me?'

She tensed, tried desperately for that insouciant armour. 'Why not?'

'Well, obviously not because you were enjoying it.'

She lifted her chin. 'How do you know I wasn't enjoying it?'

'I don't know what your experience with men has been, but most of us can tell when a woman is or isn't enjoying sex.' Luke's mouth quirked upwards even as his eyes blazed. 'Generally when a woman enjoys sex, she responds. She kisses you and makes rather nice noises. She wraps her legs around you and begs you not to stop. She doesn't lie there like a wax effigy.'

Aurelie could feel herself blushing. Her whole body felt hot. 'Maybe I thought I would enjoy it,' she threw back at him. 'Maybe you were a disappointment.'

'I have no doubt I was,' Luke returned, his tone mild. 'I confess I was a little impatient. I haven't had sex in quite a while.'

That made two of them. Aurelie swallowed. 'I don't know why we're having this conversation.'

'Because if we're going to work together for the next nine

days, I need to—' He stopped suddenly, shook his head. 'No, that's not the truth. This isn't about forging some adequate working relationship.'

Aurelie eyed him uneasily. 'What is it about, then?'

'It's about,' Luke said quietly, 'the fact that I can't stop thinking about you, or wondering how it all went so terribly wrong in the course of a single evening.'

She had no sharp retort or bantering comeback to *that*. She had no words at all. She made herself smile even though she felt, bizarrely, near tears. 'You are *so* honest.'

'Then be honest back,' Luke answered. 'Did you sleep with me to prove a point? To show me I was like all the other men you've ever known?'

'No.' It came out as no more than a whisper. Lying no longer felt like an option, not in the face of his own hard honesty. 'It was because I wanted to. Because I didn't want you to go and I…I liked being with you.' Her voice came out so low she felt the thrum of it in her chest. She stared down at her lap, wondered why anyone ever chose to be honest. It felt like peeling back your skin.

'Then what happened?' Luke asked, and his voice was low too, a gentle growl, a lion's purr.

She shrugged, her gaze still on her lap. 'Look, I've never enjoyed sex, okay? So don't worry, it wasn't an insult to your manhood or something.' She'd tried for lightness even now, and failed miserably. Luke had fallen silent, and after a few taut moments she risked a glance upwards. He was gazing at her narrowly, a crease between his eyes, as if she was a problem he had to solve.

'Never?' he finally said, and he sounded so quiet and sad that Aurelie had to blink hard.

'I wasn't abused or raped or something, if you're thinking along those lines.'

'But something happened.' It was a statement, and one

she could not deny. Yes, something had happened. Her inno-
cence had been stripped away in the course of a single evening. And she'd allowed it. But since that night she'd never
again thought of sex as something to be enjoyed. It was just
a tool, and sometimes a weapon, to get what you wanted,
or even needed.

'It doesn't matter,' she snapped. 'I don't even know why
we're talking about this. Business relationship only, remember?'

'I remember.'

'So.' She straightened, gave him an expectant this-is-your-
cue-to-leave look. He ignored it.

'Aurelie.' She wished he hadn't said her name. He said it
the way he always said it, deliberately, an affirmation, and it
made her ache inside. Stupid, because it was just her name.
A name she hated and yet—

When Luke said it, she didn't feel like Aurelie the pop
star. She felt like Aurelie the girl who'd grown up wanting
only to be loved.

'What?' she demanded, too harshly, because he'd stripped
away all her armour and anger was her last defence.

He shook his head. 'I'm sorry.'

She stared at him wordlessly, dread rolling through her,
making her sick. He was letting her down. Of course. The
concert hadn't worked and he didn't want her Aurelie act,
so he was going to tell her to go home. It was over. So much
for trying to change.

Four hours ago she'd told herself she wanted that but now
she felt the sting of tears. Another failure.

'Well,' she forced herself to say, even to smile, 'we tried,
didn't we? Never mind. I knew it was a long shot.' And she
shrugged as if it were no big deal, even managed a wobbly
laugh.

Luke frowned, said nothing for a long, taut moment. 'What do you think I'm talking about?' he finally asked.

She eyed him uncertainly. 'The concerts, right? I mean… the audience didn't really go for it today—'

'They would have if you'd done what you were supposed to, and sung your song.' He spoke without rancour, but she still prickled.

'They would have gone for it even less.'

'Yet you weren't willing to risk that. I'm sorry for that too. I should have spoken to you before you went onstage. I was trying to keep my distance because—' He stopped, blew out a weary breath. 'Because it seemed simpler. Easier. But I think I just made it harder for you. I'm sorry I let you down.' She didn't answer. This conversation had gone way outside her comfort zone. She had no comebacks, no words at all. 'But I wasn't apologising for the concerts,' Luke continued quietly. 'I'm not cancelling them. I still think you can turn this around.'

'You do?' She felt a stirring of hope, like a baby's first breath, infinitesimally small and yet sustaining life.

'Yes. But I don't want to talk about that.' He gazed straight at her then, and she saw the hard blaze of his eyes, golden glints amid the deep brown. 'I want to talk about us.'

'Us—' The word ended on a breath. She had no others.

'Yes, us. I'm still attracted to you.' Aurelie felt her heart lurch with some nameless emotion, although whether it was fear or hope or something else entirely she couldn't say.

'So it is about sex.'

Luke said nothing for a moment. He gazed out of the window, the sky turning dark, twinkling with the myriad lights of the city. 'Do you know how many women I've slept with?' he finally asked.

'I'm not sure how I would have come by that information—'

'Three.' He glanced back at her with a rueful smile, his eyes still dark. 'Three, four if I include our rather mangled attempt.'

'Right.' She had no idea what to make of that.

'I've had three relationships. *Relationships.* They all lasted months or even years. And the women involved were the only women I've ever had sex with.'

'So you really are a Boy Scout.' She felt incredibly jaded, with way too much bad experience behind her.

'No, I just…I've just always taken sex seriously. It's meant something to me. Emotionally.'

'Except with me.'

Luke was silent for so long Aurelie wondered if he'd heard her. She sought for something to say, something light and wry to show him she didn't care, it didn't matter, but it was too late for that. He'd already seen and heard too much.

'It did mean something,' he finally said, his voice so low she almost didn't hear him. 'From the moment I saw you slumped on the floor from what I thought—assumed—was an overdose. You opened your eyes and I…I felt something.'

'Felt something?' she managed, still trying for wryness. 'What, annoyance?'

'No.' He glanced up at her, and she saw the honesty blazing in his eyes. 'I don't know what it was. Is. But I can't pretend I don't feel something—for you. For the you hiding underneath the pop star persona, the you who wrote that song.'

She swallowed. 'But you didn't even hear that song until—'

'I saw it in your eyes.'

She looked away. 'I never took you for a romantic.'

'I didn't, either.'

Aurelie could feel her heart beating so hard it hurt. She felt dizzy and weirdly high, as if she were floating somewhere up near the ceiling. And she felt scared. Really scared, because she didn't know what Luke was trying to tell her.

She licked her lips, found a voice. 'So what…what are you saying exactly?'

'I don't even know.' He raked a hand through his hair, let out a weary laugh. 'Part of me thinks we should keep this strictly professional, get through the next nine days, and never see each other again.'

'That would probably be the smartest move,' she agreed, trying to keep her voice light even as her mouth dried and her heart hammered and she *hoped*. Yet for what?

'I think it would be,' Luke agreed. 'But here's the thing. I don't want to.'

'So what do you want?' Aurelie whispered.

He stared at her for a long moment, and she saw the conflict in his eyes. Felt it. He didn't want to want her, but he did. 'I want to start over,' he said at last. 'I want to forget about what happened—or didn't happen—between us. I want to get to know you properly.'

'Are you sure about that?' she joked, but her voice wavered and it fell flat.

'I'm not sure about anything,' he admitted with a wry shake of his head. 'I'm not even sure why I'm saying this.'

'Ouch. Too much honesty, maybe.'

'Maybe.' His gaze rested on her. 'But I want a second chance. With you. I want you to have a second chance with me.'

A second chance. Not professionally, but personally. So much more dangerous. And so much more desirable. A chance to be real. Aurelie closed her eyes. She didn't know what to feel, and yet at the same time she felt so much. Too much.

'The question is,' Luke asked steadily, 'is that what you want?'

She opened her eyes. Stared. His hair was still mussed, his suit still rumpled. He had shadows under his eyes and he badly needed to shave. He looked wonderful.

'Why?' she finally whispered.

'Why what?'

'Why do you want a second chance—with me?'

His mouth twisted. 'Is it so hard to believe?'

'You don't even know me.'

'I know enough to know I want to know more.'

She felt a tear, a terrible, treacherous tear, tremble on her lash. 'I would have thought,' she said in a low voice, 'that what you know would make you not want to know more.'

'Oh, Aurelie,' Luke said quietly, 'I think I know what's an act and what's real.'

'How can you know that?' She felt that tear slide coldly down her cheek. 'I don't even know that.'

'Maybe that's where I come in.'

She prickled instinctively, reached for her rusty armour. 'You think you can help me? *Save* me?'

He stilled, went silent for so long Aurelie blinked hard and looked up at him. 'No,' he said with a quiet bleakness she didn't understand. 'I know I can't save anyone.' He smiled, but it still seemed sad. 'But I can think you're worth saving. Worth knowing.'

She swallowed, sniffed. 'So what now?'

'You answer my question.' Words thickened in her throat. She didn't speak. 'Do you want to try again?' Luke asked. His gaze remained steady on her, and she found she could not look away. 'Do you want a second chance, with me?'

She couldn't speak, not with all the words thick in her throat, tangling on her tongue. Words she was desperate not to say. *Yes, but the thought terrifies me. What if you find out more about me and you hate me? What if you hurt me?*

What if it doesn't work and I feel emptier and more alone than ever? What if I can't change?

'Aurelie,' Luke said, and it wasn't a question. It sounded like an affirmation. *I know who you are.*

Except he didn't.

He was still gazing at her, still waiting. Aurelie swallowed again, tried to dislodge some of those words. She only came up with one.

'Yes,' she said.

CHAPTER SIX

LUKE STARED AT Aurelie's pale face, her eyes so wide and blue, that one tear tracking a silvery path down her cheek.

Hell.

He'd come up here to talk to her, to tell her what he'd started out saying, which was that he was sorry for what had happened but they'd keep this whole thing professional and try to avoid each other because clearly that was the safest, sanest thing to do.

Except he'd said something else instead, something totally dangerous and insane. *I know enough to know I want to know more.* No, he didn't. He didn't want to know one more thing about this impossible woman. He wanted to walk away and forget he'd ever met her.

Except that honesty thing? It got him every time. Because he knew, even as he stared at that silver tear-track on her cheek, that he'd been speaking the truth.

He felt something for her. He *did* want to get to know her, even though there could be no doubting she was fragile, damaged, *dangerous*. The possibility of hurting her was all too real—and terrifying.

'Luke?' She said his name with a soft hesitancy that he'd never heard before. She felt vulnerable, he knew. Well, hell, *he* felt vulnerable. And he didn't like it. He raked his hands through his hair, tried to find something to say.

Aurelie rose from the sofa and grabbed a tissue, her back to him as she wiped her eyes, as if even now she could hide her tears.

'Look,' she said, her back still to him, 'maybe this is a mistake.'

Luke straightened, dropped his hands. 'Why do you say that?'

She turned around. 'Because of the look on your face.'

'What—'

'You're looking like you seriously regret this whole thing.'

'I wouldn't say *seriously*.' He'd meant to joke, but she just stared at him hard. He sighed. 'Aurelie, look. This is new territory for me. I'm stumbling through the dark here.'

'You and me both.'

'Have you ever been in a serious relationship before?'

Her eyes widened, maybe with fear. 'Is that what this is?'

'No.' He spoke quickly, instinctively, and she gave him a wobbly smile. They were both scared here, both inching into this…whatever *this* was. 'One day at a time, right?' He smiled back. 'I just wondered.'

She turned away again, her hair falling in front of her face. 'You're asking because of the sex thing, right? Because I didn't enjoy it.'

'That among other things.' *The sex thing.* Yeah, that was something else they'd have to deal with. Something had happened to her, he just didn't know what. And he didn't know if he even wanted to know. His three relationships, he realised, had not prepared him for this. They'd been safe, measured, considered things, and even though he'd had a deep affection for each of the women he'd shared a part of his life with, he hadn't felt *this*.

This tangle of uncertainty and exhilaration, this terror that he could hurt her, that he might fail. What had he got himself into?

'I've been in one relationship,' she said quietly, her face still turned away from him. 'Just one. But it lasted over three years.'

'It did?' He shouldn't be surprised. He might not have seen a mention of such a relationship in the press, but he'd known from her song that she'd had her heart broken. The thought filled him with something that felt almost like jealousy.

She kept her face averted. 'I'd rather not talk about it.'

'All right.' He drew a breath, felt his way through the words. 'But if we're going to…to try this, then we need to be honest with each other.'

She let out a short laugh. 'Well, that's obviously not a problem for you.'

'Actually it is. I might be honest but that doesn't mean I wear my heart on my sleeve. No one in my family talks about emotional stuff.' And he didn't even like admitting *that*. There was a reason for his family's distance, their silence and secrets. A reason locked deep inside him.

Aurelie hunched her shoulders, folded her arms. 'Well, I'm never honest. I don't even know if I can be. I've been on my guard for so long I don't know how to let it down.' She stared at him with wide eyes. 'I honestly don't know.'

'Well, see,' Luke said lightly, 'you were being honest right there.'

She let out a shaky laugh, the sound trembling on the air. Luke felt an ache deep inside. He didn't know everything she'd been through, but he knew it had to have been a lot. And he wanted, on a deep, gut and even heart level, to make it better. To have her trust him. He wanted to redeem her, yes, maybe even save her, and save himself in the process. This time he could make it right.

'Give us a chance, Aurelie.'

'How?'

How to begin? 'We don't have to be in Singapore until the day after tomorrow. Give me tomorrow.'

She eyed him warily. 'One day?'

'One day. One date. It's a start.' For both of them.

'And then?'

'We'll see. We'll take one day at a time and see how we go.' He had a feeling one day at a time was all they could handle. He didn't know what he was asking, what he wanted. This was new territory for both of them.

'One day,' she repeated, as if she liked the sound of it. 'One date.' Luke nodded, felt his heart lift. 'Okay,' she said, and smiled.

Aurelie stood in the lobby of the hotel and tried not to fidget. Luke had told her he'd meet here at nine for their day out. Their *date*.

When had she last had a date?

She couldn't remember, although it wasn't for lack of men. There had, she knew, been far too many men in her life. But she hadn't dated them. The whole concept of a date made her feel like a giddy girl, young, innocent, full of hope.

Ha.

She was none of those things. She might only be twenty-six, but she'd lived enough for three lifetimes. And as for innocent, *hopeful*…Luke Bryant might stir something inside her she'd long thought destroyed, but he couldn't change her and she didn't think she could change herself.

And when Luke discovered that… Swallowing, she forced the fluttery panic down. There was no point thinking about the future. Luke was giving her one date. One day. And by the end of it he'd probably have had enough.

'Ready?'

She whirled around, saw Luke smiling at her. He wore a dark green polo shirt and khaki shorts, and she realised it was the first time she'd seen him in casual clothes. The shirt hugged the lean, sculpted muscles of his chest and shoulders, and the shorts rested low on his trim hips. Her gaze travelled down his tanned, muscular legs to the pair of worn trainers and then back up again to his face, where a surprising grin quirked his mouth.

'Finished?'

She had, Aurelie realised with some mortification, been checking him out. And not in a deliberate, outrageous, Aurelie-like way. No, this had been instinctive, helpless, yearning admiration. Somehow she managed to smile, nod.

'Yeah, I'm done.'

'And do I pass?'

'You'll do.'

He chuckled and placed one hand on the small of her back. She felt the warm, sure press of his palm against her skin and the answering shivers of sensation that rippled out through her body from that little touch.

'So where are we going?' she asked as they left the hotel. A luxury sedan with tinted windows and a driver at the wheel waited for them at the kerb. Luke opened the door and ushered her into the sumptuous leather interior.

'Camiguin.'

'Cami-what?'

He smiled and slid in next to her, his thigh brushing hers. Aurelie didn't know why she was suddenly hyper-aware of his movements, his body. She'd already been naked with this man; he surely shouldn't have this effect on her.

And yet, somehow, he did.

'Camiguin,' Luke repeated. 'A small island province in the Bohol Sea.'

'So we're not taking this car there, I assume?'

'No, we're taking this to the airport, and then a private

plane to Mambajao, the capital city. And then we'll hire a Jeep.'

'Planes, trains and automobiles.'

'It shouldn't take more than two hours, overall.'

'A private jet is pretty classy.'

Luke gave her the glimmer of a smile. 'I can be a pretty classy guy.'

She felt a ripple of something like pleasure at the light remark, the curve of his mouth. She'd spent so much of her time trying to push Luke away and protect herself. It felt amazingly liberating not to do it. To banter without the barbs, to relax into a—

A what? A *relationship*? She didn't do relationships. Luke might go for them, but they didn't work for her. She turned to stare out of the window, told herself this was *one date*. It was nothing. By this time tomorrow they'd probably have decided they'd *both* had enough.

The private jet was waiting for them on the tarmac at Manila's International Airport. Aurelie had taken private jets before, back in her heyday, but she hadn't been on one in over four years and it felt strange. She stood in the main cabin, glancing around at the leather sofas, the champagne chilling on ice, and felt something cold steal inside her.

Luke paused in the doorway, his gaze on her face. 'What is it?'

She glanced up at him, bemused that he would sense her mood so quickly and easily. She wasn't even sure what she was feeling. 'Nothing. Everything's very nice.'

'That's a scathing indictment if I ever heard one.' His gaze moved slowly over her, assessing, understanding. His forehead creased and he nodded. 'I guess you've taken a few of these in your time.'

She shrugged. 'One or two.'

'Does it bring back memories?'

Did it? 'No, just a feeling.'

'Not a very nice one.'

She opened her mouth to deny it, then said nothing. This honesty thing was *tough*. 'Maybe,' she finally allowed, and Luke smiled faintly, as if he knew how difficult she found this kind of talking. Sharing. All of it awkward, awful, painful.

'How have you flown under the radar for so long?'

'By holing up in Vermont.'

'And no one there gives you away?'

'They're a close-mouthed bunch. And they're loyal to my grandmother.' Too late she realised she'd said more than she meant to. Funny how that happened. You started being a little honest and then other things began to slip out. Soon she wouldn't be able to control it.

'Your grandmother? Was Julia Schmidt your grandmother, then?'

'No.' She moved over to sit on the sofa, rubbing her arms in the chilled air of the plane's interior. 'Are we going to get going?'

Luke sat across from her. 'As soon as we're cleared for take-off.' He didn't speak for a moment, just studied her, and Aurelie looked away from his gaze. She heard the plane's engines thrum to life with a feeling of relief. 'Champagne?' he asked, and she nodded, glad he wasn't going to ask any more questions.

It wasn't until he'd handed her a glass and raised his own in a toast that he finally spoke again. 'You know, this second chance thing?' She eyed him warily. 'It doesn't work if you're going to guard everything you say.'

'I wasn't,' she protested, and Luke just arched an eyebrow. She took a sip of champagne, glad for the distraction. 'I told you I'm not good at this.' He said nothing and, goaded, she said a bit sharply, 'It's not like you've been baring your soul.'

'Haven't I?' he asked quietly. He looked away then, and Aurelie felt a strange twisting inside as she thought of his words last night. Words which made a shivery thrill run all the way through her. *I know enough to know I want to know more.*

Did she want to be known?

She took a sip of champagne, the bubbles seeming to fizz all the way through her. Maybe she did. At least for one day. One date. That was safe enough, surely.

'All right.' She set her champagne glass on the coffee table between them. 'What do you want to know?'

Luke turned back to her, bemused. 'You look like you're facing the firing squad.'

'It feels that way, a little bit.'

'I suppose you've always had to be careful about what you say.'

'I haven't always been careful enough.' He acknowledged the point with a nod. There had been several tell-all exposés in various tabloids, all with too much truth in them. Aurelie felt herself start to prickle. 'So what do you want to know?'

'What do you want to tell me?'

She gave a soft laugh. 'Not much.'

'There must be something. Some small, innocuous bit of information that you don't mind imparting.'

She smiled, felt the tension inside her ease, at least a little bit. 'Well...I like bubblegum ice cream.'

'Bubblegum?' His jaw dropped theatrically. 'You have got to be kidding me.'

'It's delicious.'

'It's way too sweet—'

She leaned forward. 'And pink and sugary and with little bits of gum in the ice cream. Yum.'

'Whoa.' He held up a hand. 'TMI.'

A bubble of laughter erupted from her, surprising them

both. He smiled, a real smile, lightening his stern features in a way that made her feel suddenly breathless. His dark eyes glinted gold. She shook her head slowly. 'I didn't think you had a sense of humour, you know.'

'It's a shy creature. It only appears on rare occasions.'

'So it does.' She gazed at him thoughtfully. 'What's your favourite flavour of ice cream?'

'Not bubblegum.'

'We've established that.'

'Probably vanilla.'

'Vanilla?' She rolled her eyes. 'Could you be more boring?'

His mouth twitched. 'Probably not.'

'What's there to like about vanilla?'

'It never lets you down. Other flavours can be so disappointing. Not enough mint in the mint chocolate chip, too many nuts in Rocky Road.'

'I have been seriously disappointed, on occasion, with the lack of cookie dough in cookie dough ice cream.'

'Exactly.' He nodded his approval. 'But vanilla? Never a disappointment. Completely trustworthy.'

Like you are? She almost said the words. And meant them. No snide mockery, just truth. Too much truth. She wasn't ready for that.

'Well.' She shifted in her seat, gave him a breezy smile. 'Now we've broken the ice.'

'Or the ice cream.'

'That was a seriously weak joke.'

'I told you, my sense of humour only appears on rare occasions. Anyway—' he glanced at her as he took a sip of champagne '—can you eat bubblegum ice cream? Or does that send your glucose levels through the roof?'

'Everything in moderation.'

He nodded towards the handbag at her feet. 'I should have asked before, but did you bring everything you need?'

She nodded. 'I have a little kit for testing my blood. It travels easily.'

'When were you diagnosed?'

'When I was seventeen.' She swallowed, remembering those awful early days. At the time she'd just been moving from one event to another, dazed, incredulous, hopeful and yet still afraid.

Too late she realised Luke was watching her face, and she knew he could see the emotions in her eyes. Emotions she'd meant to hide. 'Anyway,' she said, apropos of nothing.

'How did it happen?'

'The usual symptoms. Weight loss, excessive thirst, dizzy spells.'

His eyes narrowed, and she could almost see his mind working. Understanding. 'And the tabloids claimed you had anorexia. A drinking problem. A drug overdose.'

She lifted one shoulder in a shrug. 'That's what they like to do. And in any case I haven't been a saint.' She lifted her chin a notch, tried to smile again, but her heart was thudding hard.

Luke gazed at her steadily. 'Who has?'

'You seem to have been a regular Boy Scout.'

'No, not a Boy Scout.' He rubbed his jaw, a movement that Aurelie couldn't help but notice was inherently sexy. Although, perhaps the sexiest thing about Luke Bryant was how unaware he seemed of his own attractiveness. He moved with unconscious grace, and her gaze was helplessly drawn to the shrug of his broad shoulders, the reassuring square-ness of his jaw. Everything about him solid and strong. *Safe.*

'Why haven't you ever talked about your diabetes publicly? Issued a statement?'

She leaned her head back against the seat, suddenly tired. 'It's quite a boring disease.'

'Boring?'

'Much more interesting to let them wonder. So my agent told me.'

'Your agent sucked.'

She let out a surprised laugh. 'Yeah, he wasn't that great. I fired him a couple of years ago.'

'You could have said something since then.'

She opened her eyes. 'Maybe I didn't want to.'

'Why?'

'Because telling the truth and having no one believe you is worse than not telling the truth and having people assume the worst. But I guess you wouldn't understand that,' she finished lightly, 'what with this compulsion to honesty that you have.'

Luke didn't say anything for a moment, yet Aurelie felt him tense, saw something dark flash in his eyes before he angled his head away from her. Had she inadvertently touched on something painful with her offhand remark? 'I understand,' he said finally, his voice low, and she almost asked him what he meant. She didn't, though, because they'd surely had enough honesty for one day.

By the time they arrived in Camiguin Aurelie had started feeling relaxed again. Luke had steered the conversation back to lighter subjects, moving from ice cream flavours to movie preferences and whether she supported the Mets or the Yankees.

'Mets all the way,' he'd assured her solemnly, but she saw a glint in his eyes that made her smile.

They disembarked the plane at the tiny airport and took an island taxi—basically, a rusted-out Jeep—into Mambajao. The capital of Camiguin was no more than a small town of rickety buildings with wooden verandas and tin roofs, the narrow streets bustling with bicycles and fruit vendors and raggedy children darting in and out of everything. It was so different from Aurelie's usual experience of travelling, when she kept to limos and high class hotels and never stepped outside of a severely controlled environment. She loved this. Craved the feeling of possibility and even hope wandering around the dusty streets gave her.

'What are we doing first?' she asked Luke, and he smiled and took her elbow, steering her away from a man on a bike pulling a cartload of pineapples.

'I thought we could pick up some lunch in the market, and then we'll take it out to the falls for a picnic.'

'The falls?'

'The Tuwasan Falls. They're pretty spectacular.'

'You've been there before?'

'I stopped over here the last time I came to Manila.'

She felt a completely unreasonable prickling of jealousy. Had he taken one of his serious *relationships* to this falls? Was this his go-to place for a romantic date in the tropics?

'Alone,' Luke said quietly, yet with a hint of humour in his voice that made her blush. Again. She'd never blushed so much with a man, had never had a reason to. She was Aurelie, she was worldly-wise and weary, beyond shame or embarrassment.

But that act was falling away, flaking off like old paint. What would be left when it was gone? Something good, or even anything at all? She still wasn't sure of the answer.

'Come on,' Luke said, and he guided her to a market stall overflowing with local produce and fish. 'Anything look good?'

Aurelie surveyed the jumbled piles of fruits and vegetables, the pots of noodles and trays of spring rolls.

'Crispy *pata*?' Luke suggested. 'It's deep fried pig's leg.'

She winced. 'I don't think I'm feeling quite that adventurous.'

'It's quite tasty.'

'You've had it before?'

'I like to try new things.'

She pointed to a tray of round yellowish fruit that looked a bit like potatoes. 'What's that?'

'*Lanzones.*'

'Have you had those?'

'Yes, but you have to be careful. If they're not ripe, they taste horribly sour. If they are, incredibly sweet. You just have to take your chances.' He picked up a fruit, testing its ripeness with his thumb. 'Try it.' The fruit seller quickly peeled the *lanzone* with a knife and handed her a piece. Warily, she bit into it and then, without thinking, spat the piece out into her hand. 'Yuck!'

'Bitter, huh?'

'You don't sound surprised.'

He shrugged, and she hit him in the shoulder. 'You did that on purpose!'

'Try this one.'

'Why should I trust you?' she demanded even as she took the second peeled *lanzone*.

'Because even *lanzones* deserve a second chance.'

Something in his quiet, serious tone made her mouth dry and her heart beat hard. She took a bite, and her mouth filled with the intense sweetness of the fruit. Her eyes widened. 'Wow.'

'See?' He sounded so satisfied, so smug, that Aurelie rolled her eyes.

'Thank you very much for that life lesson. Message received. Everything deserves a second chance.'

'Not everything.' After handing the vendor some coins,

he'd placed his hand on the small of her back and was guiding her to the next stall. 'Just me and the fruit.'

He acted, Aurelie thought, as if he were the only one who'd made a mistake. Who needed a second chance. Yet when she thought of her behaviour at their first meeting— and even their second—she felt as if *she* was the one who needed to change. Who wanted to prove she was different. Not Luke.

She glanced at him, her gaze taking in his stern profile, the hard line of his mouth, the latent strength of his body. What was he trying to prove?

He'd put several *lanzones* into a straw basket he'd bought from another vendor, and they added mango, spring rolls and some local sausage and cold noodles to their purchases. The sun was hot overhead even though the air felt swampy, and Luke bought two bottles of water and some sun hats as well.

'Now to the falls,' he said, and Aurelie followed him to a tin-roofed garage where he conferred with a young man who couldn't be more than sixteen before leading her around to the back where a battered-looking Jeep awaited.

'Your carriage, madam.'

She eyed it dubiously. 'I don't particularly relish breaking down in the middle of the jungle.'

'Don't worry, we're not taking this into the jungle.'

'Where, then?'

'A car park about five kilometres from here. Then we walk.'

'Walk? In the jungle?'

'It's worth it.'

'It'd better be.'

Luke stowed their provisions in the bag, handed her a sun hat, and then swung into the driver's seat. Aurelie could not keep her gaze from resting on his strong, browned forearms, the confident way he manoeuvred the rusty vehicle through the crowded streets of Mambajao and then out onto the open road, no more than a bumpy, rutted track.

The breeze was a balmy caress on her skin, the sun a benediction. In the distance the lush mountains—active volcanoes, Luke had told her—were dark, verdant humps against a hazy sky. Aurelie leaned her head back against the seat and closed her eyes.

When had she last felt this relaxed, this *happy*?

It was too long ago to remember. Smiling, she let her thoughts drift as the sunlight washed over her.

'We're here.'

She opened her eyes and saw that Luke had pulled into a rectangle of gravel and dirt that was, apparently, a car park. Their Jeep was the only car.

She rubbed her eyes. 'I must have dozed.'

'Just a little.' There was something intimate about the way he said it, and Aurelie imagined him watching her sleep. Had she rested her head on his shoulder? Had she *drooled*? More blushing.

'So where is here exactly?'

'Well, nowhere, really.' Luke slid out of the Jeep and reached for their basket. 'But we can follow a path through the jungle to the Tuwasan Falls. It's about a mile.'

'A mile in the jungle?' She glanced down at her leather sandals dubiously. 'You should have told me we were enacting *Survivor*.'

He made a face. 'Sorry. But it's mostly wooden walkways, so I think you'll be okay.'

'If you say so.'

She followed him away from the car park and onto exactly what he'd said—a wooden walkway on stilts over the dense jungle floor. Within just a few metres of going down the walkway she felt the air close around her, hot, humid and dense. Birds chirped and cicadas chirruped—at least she thought they were cicadas—and she could feel the jungle like a living, breathing entity all around her. A bright green lizard scampered across the walkway, and in the distance some animal—Aurelie had no idea what—gave a lonely, mournful cry.

'Wow.' She stopped, her hands resting on the cane railings, her heart thumping. 'This is…intense.'

Luke glanced back at her. 'You okay?'

'Yes, I guess I just thought, you know, first date, maybe a movie?'

He smiled wryly. 'I know you think I'm boring, but Jeez. A movie? I think I can do better than that.'

'I don't think you're boring.'

'You think I'm the human equivalent of vanilla ice cream.'

She gazed at him, the railings slick under her palms. Her heart was still thumping. 'I do,' she admitted quietly, and it felt like the most honest thing she'd ever said. 'Completely trustworthy.'

Luke's eyes darkened and the moment spun out between them, a thread of silence that bound them together, and tighter still. 'Don't speak too soon,' he finally said, and turned away from her to walk further down the path.

'You mean you're not?'

'I mean you don't trust me yet, and why should you? It's something I have to earn.'

Despite the damp heat all around them her mouth felt dry. She swallowed. 'And you want to earn it?'

He glanced back at her, and his eyes were darker than ever. 'Yes.'

Her mind spun with this revelation. She wanted to tell him that he'd already earned it, that she trusted him now, but somehow the words wouldn't come.

They didn't talk for a little while after that, because the

wooden walkway became decidedly rickety, and then it stopped altogether at the bank of a rushing stream.

Aurelie raised her eyebrows. 'What now, Tarzan?'

'We cross it.'

'Did I mention my leather sandals?'

'You might have.'

'And?'

'I didn't think you were the type to care about shoes.'

She wasn't. 'No, but I'm the type to care about getting my big toe eaten by a giant barracuda.'

He laughed then, a great big rumbling laugh that had a silly grin spreading wide across her face. She liked the sound of his laughter. 'I don't think there are any giant barracudas.'

'No?'

'Only medium-sized ones.'

She pursed her lips, hands firmly planted on her hips. 'Is that your sense of humour appearing on this rare occasion?'

'Oops, it darted away again.' He stepped onto a flattish rock in the stream, the water flowing all around him, and stretched out his hand. 'Come here.'

Cautiously she reached out and put her hand in his. His clasp was dry, warm and firm, and with his other hand on her arm he helped her onto the rock. Their hips bumped. Heat flared.

'This is cosy,' she murmured and he gave a tiny smile.

'That's the idea. Next rock.'

He stepped backwards onto another rock, sure and agile, and Aurelie followed him. She could hear the water rushing past them, felt the warm spray of it against her ankles. In the middle of the stream she looked down and saw a bright blue fish darting very near her toes. She slipped and Luke slid an arm around her waist, balanced her. Easily.

'The secret is not to look down.'

'Now you tell me.'

Another rock, and then another, and then they were on the other side. Luke smiled at her rather smugly, and Aurelie shook her head.

'This is all a big lesson, isn't it? How to Trust 101.'

'Is it working?'

'A little,' she admitted. 'What if I'd fallen?'

'But you didn't.'

'But what if I had? What if you'd slipped?'

'Me? Slip?' He shook his head, then gazed at her, his head tilted to one side. 'Do you think it would have ruined everything?'

Her lips curved. She liked being with this man. 'Not everything. But after the *lanzone*…'

'It was delicious.'

'The second one.'

'Exactly.'

He hadn't let go of her hand, and now he led her alongside the stream, the ground soft and loamy beneath them. Aurelie found she quite liked the feel of his fingers threaded through hers. They walked along the bank, winding their way up through the dense foliage, until Luke stopped suddenly.

'Close your eyes.'

More trust. 'Okay.' She closed her eyes and felt Luke tug on her hand. She took a step. Another.

'Open them,' he said softly, and she did. And gasped in wonder.

CHAPTER SEVEN

'Wow.'

'Definitely worth it, huh?'

She turned from the stunning view of the falls to Luke's rather smug smile. 'I wouldn't say definitely. I think my sandals are ruined.'

'Leather dries.'

'It is amazing,' she admitted and his smile widened. Not so smug, she decided. More like...satisfied. *Happy.*

'Let's find a place for a picnic.' He tugged on her hand again and they picked their way along the rocks until they found a large flat one, warm from the sun and perfect for a picnic.

Aurelie stretched out on top of it as Luke unpacked their lunch, her gaze on the waterfall once more. It truly was a spectacular sight, a crystalline fountain flowing from the fern-covered rocks, falling in a sparkling stream to a tranquil pool fifty feet or more below.

She turned to watch Luke peel a *lanzone* with a knife. He glanced up, smiling, a decidedly wicked glint in his eyes. 'Care to try another?'

'I don't know if I dare.'

'This one's sweet, I promise.' And with that wicked glint still in his eyes he fed her a chunk of the sweet, moist fruit, his fingers brushing her lips as she ate it. The barest touch

of his fingers against her mouth sent little pulses of aware-
ness firing through her, flaring deep down. *Desire.* It seemed
amazing that she could feel it. Want it—and him. She'd never
wanted anyone before, not like that. Not since Pete.

'Tasty,' she managed, and swiped at the droplets of juice
on her lips. Her heart rate was skittering all over the place,
and all from that simple touch and the feelings and thoughts
it had triggered, a maelstrom swirling through her.

'You know,' she said as Luke arranged the rest of their
picnic items onto two paper plates, 'I don't really know anything about you.'

'What do you want to know?'

'Something. Anything. Where did you grow up?'

'New York City and Long Island.'

'The Hamptons?' He nodded, and she hugged her knees to
her chest. 'I guess you grew up pretty privileged, huh? Bryant Enterprises and all that?' She didn't know much about
the Bryant family, but she knew they were rich. Featured
in the society pages rather than the trashy tabloids like her.
'And you have a brother, you mentioned?'

'Two.'

'Are you close?'

'No.' Luke spoke mildly enough, but Aurelie sensed a dark
current of emotion swirling underneath the words, a tension
and repressiveness. She was getting to know this man, and
now she wanted to understand him.

'Why aren't you?'

He lifted one shoulder in a shrug. 'The short answer? Because Aaron's an ass and Chase checked out a long time ago.'

'Those are rather nice alliterations, but what does that
really mean?'

Luke sighed and sat back, his arms braced on the rock
behind him. 'It means my older brother, Aaron, loves to be
the boss. I can't really blame him, because my father encour-

aged it, told him he was going to be CEO of Bryant Enterprises when he was older, and he needed to be responsible, authoritative, et cetera. Let's just say Aaron got the message.'

Aurelie observed the tightening of Luke's mouth, his eyes narrowed as he gazed out at the falls, the sunlight catching the spray and causing it to glitter.

'And Chase?'

'Chase is my younger brother. He was always a rebel, got in trouble loads of times, expelled from boarding school, the whole bit. My father disinherited him when he was in college.'

'Ouch.'

'I don't know if Chase even cared. He made his own fortune as an architect and he hardly ever gets in touch.'

Aurelie hugged her knees. 'That's sad.'

'Is it?' He glanced at her, eyebrows raised. 'Maybe he's better off. When I do see him, he always seems happy. Joking around.'

'Maybe that's his schtick.'

'Maybe.'

'And what about you?' Aurelie asked quietly, because that was what she really wanted to know. 'Where did you fit into that picture?' Luke hesitated, and she knew she was getting closer to understanding. 'Or didn't you?'

'I suppose I was the classic middle child.'

'Which is?'

'Caught between two larger personalities. As we got older we all drifted apart and that seemed easier.'

'It doesn't sound like a very comfortable place.'

'No, I don't suppose it was.' Luke turned to her with a faint smile, although Aurelie could still sense that dark emotion swirling underneath. 'I don't miss my childhood, at any rate. I was shy, awkward, and I even had a stammer.' He spoke lightly, but it didn't matter. Aurelie knew it hurt. 'My father didn't have much time for me, to tell you the truth.' He glanced away. 'He didn't have time for me at all.'

'Sounds a bit like my childhood,' Aurelie answered quietly.

Luke turned back to her, his gaze sharp now, eyes narrowed in concern. 'Oh? How so?'

She swallowed past the ache that had started in her throat, an ache of sympathy and remembrance. She'd never told anyone about her childhood. In the world of celebrity, it held a touch too much pathos to be interesting. 'Well, my mother didn't have much time for me. And my father wasn't in the picture.'

'Who raised you?' That thoughtful crease appeared between his brows. 'Your grandmother?'

'I wish. I only stayed a summer with her, when I was eleven, but it was the happiest time of my life.'

'Then where did you grow up?'

'Nowhere. Everywhere. My mom never stayed in the same place for more than a few months, sometimes a few weeks. She'd get a job in a local diner or something, enrol me in school and find a deadbeat boyfriend. When he started stealing her money or knocking her around, she'd move on, dragging me with her.'

'That's terrible,' Luke said quietly, and Aurelie shrugged. 'I got over it.'

'Julia Schmidt,' he said after a moment. 'Your mother. You bought the house from her, didn't you?'

She nodded. 'When my grandmother died she left it to my mom. I was only seventeen, and I think she hoped it would help my mom settle down.'

'But?'

Aurelie sighed. 'My mom didn't want to settle down. So I bought the house from her for far more than it was worth. I was famous by then, so I had the money.'

'And you finally had a home.'

She blinked hard, amazed at how quickly and easily he understood her. How in this moment it felt good and right and safe, rather than scary.

'It must have been a huge loss when your grandmother died,' he said after a moment, and she nodded.

'I still miss her.'

'And your mother?'

A shrug. 'Around. Who knows? She used to appear every so often asking for money, but now that I'm not in the spotlight any more—at least not for any good reason—she's disappeared.' She sighed and stretched out her legs. 'She'll surface one day, I'm sure.'

'So you really are alone.'

So alone. Although she didn't feel alone right now. She wanted to tell him that, confess just a little of the happiness in her heart that he'd helped to create, but fear held her back. Rejection was still a distinct and awful possibility. There was still so much Luke didn't know.

'What about your parents? Are they around?'

He shook his head. 'Both dead.'

'I'm sorry.' Aurelie gazed at him, saw how he'd carefully schooled his features into a completely neutral mask. 'How did they die?'

'My father of a heart attack when I'd just finished college.' A pause, a telling hesitation. 'My mother developed breast cancer when I was thirteen.'

'I'm sorry. That's terrible.'

He jerked his head in a semblance of a nod, his face still so very neutral. He was holding something back, Aurelie suspected, some pain that he didn't want to share with her. She decided not to press.

'So you're alone too,' she said quietly and after a taut moment of silence Luke reached for her hand.

'Not right now,' he said, and as Aurelie's heart turned right over he tugged her to her feet. 'Let's swim.'

'Swim?' Aurelie eyed the deep, tranquil pool below the falls with a dubious wariness. 'What about the giant barracudas?'

'You mean the medium-sized ones? They're friendly.'

'I didn't bring a swimsuit.'

'I'm sure we can improvise.' She hesitated and Luke added quietly, 'Unless you don't want to.'

Was this another trust exercise? she wondered. She was so used to men seeing her as an object. A trophy. She'd encouraged it, after all. And yet she knew Luke was different, knew he saw her differently.

'Okay,' she said. 'Let's do it.'

Luke led her down a narrow path to the pool. Aurelie tilted her head up to watch the waterfall cascade down the rock, churning foam that emptied into a surprisingly placid pool.

'Good thing you're not shy any more,' she said as Luke tugged his shirt over his head. Then her mouth dried, for the sight of his bare chest was glorious enough to start her heart thumping. His shoulders were broad, his chest powerful and browned and perfectly taut. Washboard abs, trim hips. She was gaping like a fool, and realised it when Luke gave her a knowing grin and dropped his shorts.

He wore boxers, and Aurelie could not draw her gaze away from his powerful thighs. As for what was hidden beneath the boxers…

'Look at me like that much longer and I'm going to embarrass myself,' Luke said, a thread of humour in his voice although she caught the ragged note of desire too. And it thrilled her.

She wasn't sure how it could feel so different from before, when she'd wielded his desire for her like a weapon. Now it felt like a joy. She glanced up and smiled right into his eyes.

'I don't think that would necessarily be a bad thing.'

He nodded towards her pale pink sundress. 'Your turn.'

He'd already seen her naked. He'd seen her in her skimpy Aurelie underwear several times. Yet this felt different too, more honest, more bare. She slid the straps from her shoulders and shrugged out of the dress.

'Sorry. I'm wearing boring underwear.' Just a plain cotton bra and boy shorts. Really, incredibly modest. Yet she felt nearly naked, and her body responded to Luke's heated gaze, an answering heat flaring within her, stirring up all sorts of wants. As well as just a tiny little needle of fear. No, not fear, but uncertainty. Memory.

Luke smiled and turned towards the pool. 'Last one in,' he called, and dived neatly into the water below. Aurelie watched him surface, sluicing the water from his face, clearly enjoying himself. He glanced up at her. 'Is a rotten egg,' he finished solemnly and she laughed. Still didn't move.

'Are you chicken?'

'I prefer the word cautious.' She hadn't swum in anything but a lap pool in years.

'Didn't you swim in a lake or watering hole that summer you spent in Vermont?' Luke called up to her. 'This is no different. In fact, it's nicer because the bottom is sand and rock rather than squishy mud.'

She stared at him, amazed at how much he guessed. Knew. She had swum in a lake in Vermont, a muddy-bottomed pond that she'd spent hours in.

'Come on,' Luke called. 'I'm right here. I promise you can scramble onto my shoulders if a medium-sized barracuda happens by.'

More trust. Funny, how trusting in these silly little things made her start to unbend to the notion of trusting him with the bigger things. Like the truth. No, she'd been honest enough about her past for one afternoon. But this she could do.

Taking a deep breath, she took a running jump into the pool. The water closed over her head and for a moment she remained below the surface, treading water and enjoying the complete stillness and silence until she felt Luke's hands close around her shoulders and he hauled her upwards.

'What—'

'You want to scare me to death?' he demanded, but she saw that telltale glint in his dark eyes. 'I thought you were drowning.'

'I can swim, you know.'

'Maybe one of those barracudas had got you.'

She laughed, but the sound trembled and died on her lips as she saw Luke's eyes darken, his pupils dilate, and she felt the pulse of desire in herself. He still held her by the shoulders, and she was close enough to see the droplets of water clinging to his skin, the enticing curve of his mouth, a mouth that she knew was soft and warm and delicious.

Then Luke let her go, easing away from her, and struck out towards the falls. 'Come see this,' he called over his shoulder, and Aurelie felt a flicker of disappointment. Had she wanted him to kiss her?

Yes, she had.

How novel. How exciting. How disappointing that he hadn't.

With a little shake of her head, she swam over to join him at the waterfall.

'There's a little cave behind the falls,' Luke explained. 'Just swim underneath the waterfall and you'll come up right into it.'

'Okay.'

Luke dived down first and Aurelie followed him, surfacing a few seconds later into a shallow fern-covered overhang, the waterfall a sparkling crystalline curtain hiding them from the world. Luke hauled himself up onto a ledge and extended a hand to her.

They sat side by side in silence for a moment, and to Aurelie it seemed completely relaxed, completely wonderful. She'd never felt so much in accord with another human being before, and she knew she wanted to tell him. Forget the fear. Screw rejection. This was too incredible, too important.

She turned to him with a smile. 'It's amazing. This whole day has been amazing.'

Luke touched her cheek, no more than a brush of his fingers. 'It has been for me too.' His gaze was tender and yet intent on hers, the curve of his mouth so close—

'Luke—' She wasn't sure what she was going to say. *Kiss me,* maybe, because she wanted him to. Desperately. But he didn't. Didn't even let her finish, just slipped off the ledge and swam underneath the falls once more.

With a little sigh Aurelie followed him.

They swam a bit more in the shallows of the pool, splashing, teasing and laughing and finally they got out and returned to the sun-warmed rock to dry.

Aurelie sat there, her arms braced behind her, her legs stretched out, wearing only her underwear. And felt completely natural, no Aurelie artifice or armour. She was, she knew, being herself; she'd been herself for nearly the whole day. There *was* something there, underneath all the posing, and she'd needed Luke to show her.

'So if your mother was dragging you around in pursuit of her deadbeats, how did you actually become famous?' Luke asked after they'd sat in a comfortable silence for a little while.

'At a karaoke night at a bar in Kansas, if you can believe it,' Aurelie answered.

'You sang karaoke?'

'We both did. It was a mother-daughter thing.'

'Ah.'

'What do you mean, *ah*?' she asked, because he sounded as if she'd just said something significant.

'Well, your mother isn't famous, is she?'

'No—'

'I'll bet she wasn't pleased that her teenage daughter—how old were you, sixteen?'

'Fifteen,' Aurelie said softly. 'It was a month before my sixteenth birthday.'

'Young and gorgeous,' Luke stated, 'and about to be famous. And your mother wasn't any of those things.'

Strange, she'd never thought of it that way. She'd never considered that her mother might have been jealous of her. Yet now, looking back on that fateful, life-altering night, she remembered how quiet her mother had been. Of course, Pete had done all the talking, made his promises, told Aurelie she was going to be a star. She swallowed, willing the memories away. It had begun right there, she knew, the destruction of herself. The building up of Aurelie.

'It's hard to remember, isn't it,' Luke said quietly. 'I'm sorry.'

She shook her head, her throat tight. 'In some ways it was the happiest—well, I felt the happiest then than I had in such a long time. But if I'd known, if anyone could have told me—'

'Told you what?'

She swallowed. Here was the honesty that hurt. 'That I'd lose my soul. That I'd sell it, because I didn't even know what I was giving away.'

Luke frowned. 'I suppose fame will do that to you.'

'It wasn't fame. It was—' She stopped because she didn't want to tell him, didn't even know how. 'It was awful,' she finished quietly.

He was silent for a long moment. '"Never give your heart

away,"' he quoted her song softly. 'Is that what happened, Aurelie? Someone broke your heart?'

She swallowed. 'Yes.'

He nodded, sorrowfully understanding. 'Three years is a long time. It must have hurt when it was over.'

She let out a sudden, hard laugh because Luke had completely the wrong idea and she didn't want to have to correct him. 'It felt like forever,' she agreed after a moment. 'But my heart didn't break when it was over, Luke. It broke when it began.'

CHAPTER EIGHT

IT BROKE WHEN it began.

Aurelie had said the words with such flat finality, such aching sorrow, that Luke knew she meant them. He just didn't know what they meant.

'I don't understand,' he said quietly, but she shook her head.

'I don't want to talk about it. I don't want to ruin this perfect day by bringing all that up. And it has been perfect, Luke. Everything.' She gazed at him with those wide rain-washed eyes and Luke felt everything in him twist and yearn.

He'd wanted to kiss her so many times today. When she'd planted her hands on her hips and given him an impish look, when she'd tossed him a teasing glance, when he'd held her in the water and longed to pull her close, their wet limbs sliding over each other, twining around.

Hell, he'd been in a permanent state of arousal, it seemed, for half the day. Yet he'd kept his distance, and he would now, because this wasn't about desire.

It was about trust.

He'd meant what he said about earning it. He'd let her down before, but he wouldn't again. He had, despite his instinct which insisted there was so much more, taken her at face value. Aurelie the go-to-hell pop star. And he'd allowed her to seduce him, allowed himself to give in to his own need because the desire had been so strong. Only when he had seen the pain on her face, written on her heart, and known he'd shown her he was just like all the others, had he been able to stop. Yet he feared the damage had been done.

It broke when it began.

What did she mean? Had some bastard abused her? The sudden strong urge to kill such a man with his bare hands surprised him. Aurelie aroused all sorts of feelings in him, feelings he hadn't had in a long time. He had, he saw now, been skimming through life, never going too deep, using work as an excuse because this—this emotion, this intensity—was frightening. Reminded him of how much you could lose, how much risk and pain was involved in any real relationship.

Not pain for him—he didn't care about that—but pain for her. He didn't want to hurt her, and he was so afraid that he might.

How did your parents die?

For a second, no more, he'd wanted to tell her the truth. Yet honesty only went so far, and that secret was buried so deep inside him he didn't think he could let it out if he tried. He tried not to think about it, yet being with this woman brought his own secrets swimming upwards to the light, just like hers.

They were *both* being real.

'It has been perfect,' he agreed. 'But it's getting late and we've got a mile trek through the jungle as well as a ride in the Jeep and a plane to catch.'

'Back to reality,' Aurelie said, making a face, and Luke reached for her hand.

'Maybe reality won't be so bad,' he said quietly. This new reality, with the two of them in it together. *One day at a time.* Yet what would tomorrow hold?

They walked back to the Jeep in companionable silence,

the jungle lush and vibrant all around them. As they emerged into the sunlight a brilliant blue morpho butterfly fluttered close to Aurelie's face and briefly alighted on her hair. She laughed aloud, and Luke smiled to see her joy. Then suddenly, impulsively perhaps, she leaned over and brushed her lips against his.

He stilled under that little kiss, felt a flare of heat inside, the instant arousal, yet something more. Something precious, because he knew that little kiss hadn't been calculated. It had been an expression of her heart.

'What was that for?' he asked, and she shrugged, smiling.

'Just because I wanted to.' She paused, bit her lip. 'Do you mind?'

Mind? 'No,' Luke said. 'I don't mind at all.'

'Good.'

And that, he knew, was a very good start.

By the time they got on the plane Aurelie was feeling sleepy. She curled up in a corner of one of the leather sofas, and when Luke came and sat down right beside her it felt amazingly natural to rest her head on his shoulder. Luke curved his arm around her, drew her closer so her cheek rested against his chest, and with a kind of wonderful incredulity Aurelie realised that felt natural too. It felt right. She snuggled closer, and by the time the plane took off her eyes were drifting shut.

They got back to the hotel after dark, and Luke walked her all the way to the door of her suite. Aurelie turned to him, felt her heart throw itself against her ribs. Should she ask him to come in? Did she want him to? Part of her did, desperately, and another part still felt that old fear.

She took out her keycard, hesitated and turned to Luke. 'Well.' She swallowed, smiled. Sort of.

Luke smiled back and cupped her cheek. The feel of his warm palm against her skin was both reassuring and exciting. Yet even so Aurelie felt herself tensing. She wanted this, she did, and yet…

'Goodnight, Aurelie.' Luke dropped his hand and turned to walk back down the corridor. Aurelie stared at him in disbelief, a little disappointment.

'You mean you aren't…you aren't going to kiss me?'

Luke glanced back, eyes glinting. 'No.'

'But—'

'You didn't want me to.'

'I did,' she said, but she knew she didn't sound that convincing.

'Maybe,' Luke suggested quietly, 'you didn't know what you wanted. And until you do, completely, I'm not going to touch you.'

Aurelie stared at him, her mind spinning. 'Why not?'

'I think the better question is, why would I?' She had no answer to that one. With one last smile Luke walked down the hallway and left her there, half-wishing he'd kissed her and half-glad he hadn't.

The next morning dawned hot and bright and Aurelie lay in bed, her mind tumbling over the events of yesterday—including Luke's non-kiss—and then suddenly freezing on the realisation of what today was.

Today they travelled to Singapore, and she was giving another concert for the store opening tonight. Swallowing hard, she drew her knees up to her chest and hugged them tight. Somehow she didn't think her fans in Singapore wanted to hear her new song any more than the ones in the Philippines had. Which left her…where?

She avoided the question as she got dressed and ate breakfast, meeting Luke down in the lobby at nine, as they'd agreed earlier. They were taking his private jet to Singapore, and from there going on to the Fullerton Bay Hotel on Marina Bay. They'd check in and go directly to Bryant's.

By the time she'd boarded Luke's jet Aurelie could no longer ignore the fluttering nerves that were threatening to take her over. She glanced at Luke sitting across from her, a sheaf of papers on his lap, his thumb and forefinger bracing his temple. He looked so serious and stern, and yet a lock of unruly dark hair had fallen across his forehead and Aurelie longed to brush it away, to savour its softness under her fingers. She'd been wanting to touch him more and more. Luke was awakening a desire in her she hadn't thought she possessed, and all by *not* touching her.

Yet what would happen when he did?

He glanced up as if aware of her gaze, smiled ruefully. 'You're nervous.'

For a stunned second she thought he'd guessed the nature of her thoughts, then realised with some relief that he was talking about the concert. 'Yes, I am.'

'You'll be fine.'

'You don't know that.'

'True.' He stretched his legs in front of him and put the papers back in a leather case. 'What did you do when you had all those big concerts? To warm up, I mean, and get rid of stage fright?'

Aurelie shrugged. 'Honestly, I don't know. I didn't really have stage fright.'

Luke arched an eyebrow. 'Never? Not even when you played to ten thousand people in Madison Square Garden?'

She laughed, but the sound trembled. 'No, because it was all an act. It wasn't really me, and so I didn't…I didn't really care.'

'And now it's you, and you care,' he finished softly, and she nodded, stared at her hands. Luke covered her hand with his own, twined his fingers through hers. He didn't say anything, didn't offer false promises about how they'd all love her, and she was glad. Silence could be honest too.

Yet her nervousness came back as they landed in Singapore and took a limo to the hotel. Aurelie barely registered the sumptuous suite with its view of the bay from one balcony and the city skyline from the other. All she could think about was how in just a few hours she would walk onto that stage and bare her soul.

Why had she written the damn song, anyway? And why had she ever played it for Luke?

'It doesn't matter what they think, you know,' Luke said. She turned and saw him standing in the doorway of her suite. 'It doesn't mean anything if they don't like it.'

'Doesn't it?'

'No. What matters is what you think of it. How you think of yourself.'

How she thought of herself? She couldn't answer that one. Being herself still felt so new, so strange. She still wasn't sure she even knew who she was.

'We'd better get going,' she said, and slipped past him out into the corridor.

Luke stayed with her as they toured the store, five floors on Orchard Road, and showed her the new café, the glittering beauty hall, the department for crafts and clothing all supplied by local artisans, clearly his brain child.

'Don't you have important people to see?' she asked, half-joking, as he escorted her to the dressing room where she was to get ready. Already people were milling about the marble lobby, waiting for the official opening.

'I'll check in with a few people now, and come back before you go on.'

Aurelie swallowed. Luke had done a good job of distracting her with the tour, but the fear—the *terror*—was now coming back in full force.

'Okay,' she said, still trying for insouciance and failing miserably. He put his hands, strong and comforting, on her shoulders and smiled down at her.

'Forget about the crowd,' he said quietly. 'Forget about me. Sing your song for yourself, Aurelie. You need that.'

Somehow, despite the tears now stinging her eyes, she dredged up a smile. 'I knew this was pity,' she joked, and he pressed his lips to her forehead.

'You can do it. I know you can.'

And then he was gone, and Aurelie sagged against the door, completely spent from that small encounter.

By the time Luke returned half an hour later she was ready—or at least as ready as she'd ever be. She wore a sundress this time, in a soft, cloud-coloured lavender, and cowboy boots. Her hair fell tousled to her shoulders, and she carried her guitar.

Luke smiled. 'You look fantastic.'

She smiled back, wobbly and watery. 'I feel like complete crap.'

'You can do it,' he said, and this time it wasn't an encouragement, it was a statement. He believed in her. More, perhaps, than she believed in herself.

A few minutes later she was miked and ready to go, and then she was on. She heard the hiss of indrawn breath as she walked onstage. Another surprised, perhaps even outraged, audience. She sat on the stool, stared into the faceless crowd. Swallowed. Her heart hammered so hard it hurt, and she felt a blind panic overwhelm her like a fog. She couldn't do this.

Then she felt Luke's presence on the side of the stage, just a few feet away. Strange, impossible even, to feel someone when he didn't move or speak, yet she did. He felt warm, and his warmth melted away the fog. She glanced sideways, saw his steady gaze, his smile. She took a breath. Blinked. And started to play.

Distantly she heard the rippled murmur of confusion as she began to play a song they didn't recognise. Her song. But then the song took over and she knew it didn't matter what anyone in the audience thought. Luke had been right; she wasn't doing this for them. She wasn't doing it just for herself, either.

She was doing it for him. Because he was the one person who had believed in her, more than she'd been able to believe in herself. Already he'd given her back her soul; he'd shown her how to reclaim it. She played the song for him, for her, for *them*.

And when it was over and the last note faded away, you could have heard a pin drop on the marble floor of the lobby. You could have heard the tiniest sigh, because no one did anything. No one clapped.

They didn't, Aurelie knew numbly, know *what* to do with her. How to react.

Then, from the side of the stage, she heard the sound of someone clapping. Loudly. *Luke.* And the sound of his clapping was like the trigger to an avalanche, and suddenly everyone was clapping. Aurelie sat there, her guitar held loosely in one hand, blinking in the bright lights and smiling like crazy. And crying too, at least she was as she walked offstage and straight into Luke's arms.

He enveloped her in a tight hug, his lips against her hair. 'You did it. I knew you could.'

She tried to speak, but there was too much emotion lodged in a hot lump in her throat, too many tears in her eyes. So she did what she wanted to do, what she needed to do. She kissed him.

This wasn't a tentative brush of her lips against his. She kissed him with all the passion and hope, the gratitude and joy that she felt. She dropped her guitar and wrapped her arms around him, and Luke took her kiss and made it his own, kissing her back with all he felt too.

It was, Aurelie thought dazedly, the most wonderful kiss.

The rest of the evening passed in a happy blur. Luke kept her by his side, introducing her to various officials and dignitaries, and for once in her life Aurelie didn't feel like the pop star performing for another sceptical crowd. No, with Luke next to her, she simply felt like herself. A woman whose hand was being held by a handsome and amazing man.

She was, Aurelie thought distantly, halfway to falling in love with him. It didn't seem possible after such a short time, and yet she felt the truth of it inside her, like a flame that had ignited to life. She never wanted it to go out.

And yet what *did* she want? The memory of that passionate kiss by the side of the stage had seared itself into her senses, but she still felt her insides jangle with nerves at the thought of what else could happen. What she wanted to happen...and yet was afraid of, both at the same time.

Despite her wonder and worry about what might happen later, she still enjoyed every minute of the evening spent by Luke's side. A dinner for the VIP guests had been arranged in the conservatory on top of the store, with the lights of Singapore stretched out in a twinkling map on three sides, and the bay with its bobbing yachts and sailing boats on the other. A silver sickle moon hung above them, and she felt the warm pressure of Luke's hand on the small of her back.

'Are you having a good time?'

'Very.' She turned to smile at him. 'You've done an amazing job with all these openings. I've heard a lot of great things about the new design of the store.'

'I've heard a lot of great things about your new song.'

She let out a little laugh. 'If you hadn't started clapping, I'm not sure anyone would have.'

'They would have. They just needed a little nudge.'

'Maybe next time you should hold up cue cards. Flash "Clap" in big letters as soon as I finish.'

'Next time they'll know. There were a lot of media people out there in the audience tonight. Word will get around.'

She drew a deep breath and let it out rather shakily. 'That's a scary thought.'

'Is it?'

'I don't know what the response will be.'

'Does it matter?'

She stared at him, surprised, until she realised it *didn't* matter. She hadn't written or performed the song to impress people or even make them change their minds about her. She didn't even want a comeback. She wanted...this.

Acceptance and understanding of who she was, not by a faceless crowd or the world at large, but by Luke—and by herself. And somehow he'd known that even before she had.

'Come on,' he said, 'I have some people I want you to meet.' And with his hand still on her back he guided her through the room.

Luke watched Aurelie chat and laugh with the CEO of the Orchard Bank of Singapore and felt something inside him swell. He loved her like this, natural and friendly and free. He loved *her*.

The thought, sliding so easily into his mind, made him still even as he attempted to keep involved in the conversation. He was trying to negotiate a new deal with a local clothes retailer to design exclusively for Bryant's. It would be an important agreement, and he couldn't afford to insult the CEO across from him.

And yet...he loved her? After just a few short days? When he still couldn't really say he knew her, not the way he'd known the three women with whom he'd had significant relationships. They'd dated for years, had known each other's peeves and preferences, had run their relationship like a well-oiled machine. And yet now he felt he could barely remember their faces. Had he loved them? Not like this, maybe not at all. He'd been emotionally engaged, certainly, although it hadn't hurt that much when they'd mutually agreed to end it.

But this? Her? It felt completely different. Completely overwhelming and intoxicating and scary. Was that love? Did he want it, if it was?

Did he have a choice?

And could she love him, when there were things he hadn't told her? Failures and weaknesses he hadn't breathed a word about? His insides clenched at the thought. She'd been slowly and deliberately baring herself—her soul, her secrets—while he'd kept his firmly locked away.

Could love exist with that kind of imbalance?

'Mr Bryant?'

Too late Luke realised he hadn't heard a word the man in front of him had said. He swallowed, tried to smile.

'I'm sorry?'

Several hours later Luke found Aurelie laughing with the wife of a foreign diplomat and placed a proprietorial hand on the small of her back. He liked being able to touch her in this small way, even if the ways he really wanted to touch her—had been dreaming of touching her—were still off-limits. He'd told her he wouldn't touch her until she wanted him to, until she was certain, and he knew she wasn't yet. He saw the shadows in her eyes even when she was smiling.

'I'm sorry to steal Aurelie away from you,' he told the woman, 'but we have a full day tomorrow and she needs her rest.' He smiled to take any sting from the words, and the woman nodded graciously. 'Been having a nice time?' he asked Aurelie as they headed down to the limo he had waiting.

'Amazing, actually. I thought it would be completely boring, but it wasn't.'

'That's refreshingly honest.'

She laughed, the sound unrestrained, natural. 'Sorry, I didn't mean to be insulting. It's just I've gone to so many parties and receptions and things and it's always been so exhausting.'

'Another performance.'

'Exactly. But it wasn't tonight. I was just able to be myself.' She shook her head slowly. 'I never thought that playing my song would give me anything but a kind of vindication that I could be something other than a pop star, but it has. It's made me feel like I can be myself…anywhere. With anyone.' She paused before adding softly, 'With you.'

She gazed up at him with those wide stormy-sea eyes and Luke felt that insistent flare of lust. He wanted her so badly. His palms itched with the need to slide down the satiny skin of her shoulders, fasten on her hips. Draw her to him and taste her sweetness.

She must have seen something of that in his face because her tongue darted out to moisten her lips and she took a hesitant step closer to him. 'Luke—'

He didn't know what he might have done then, if he would have taken her in his arms just as he'd imagined and wanted, but then the doors pinged open and a crowd of guests moved aside to let them pass. Luke let out a shaky breath and led Aurelie towards the limo.

They didn't speak in the intimate darkness of the car, but he felt the tension coiling between and around them. Felt her thigh press against his own when the limo turned a curve, and the length of his leg felt as if it had been dusted with a shower of sparks. He heard, as if amplified, every draw and sigh of her breath, the thud of his own heart.

He hadn't felt this overwhelmed by desire since he'd been

about eighteen. He let out another audible, shaky breath and stared blindly out of the window.

They remained silent as the limo pulled in front of the hotel, and then in the lift up to their separate suites on the same floor. Luke took out his keycard; it was slick in his hand. His mouth had dried but he forced himself to speak. To sound as if he were thinking of anything other than hauling Aurelie into his arms and losing himself deep inside her.

'So. Another big day tomorrow.'

'Is it? What's the schedule exactly?'

Was he imagining that she sounded just a little breathless? Her cheeks were flushed, her eyes bright. She tucked a strand of hair behind her ear, and Luke's gaze was irresistibly drawn to the movement, the curve of her ear and the elegant line of her neck.

He swallowed. 'We fly to Hong Kong, spend a day touring the city with some officials and then have the opening on the following day, along with a reception. Then two days' rest and on to Tokyo.'

'Right.' She glanced away, and the lift doors swooshed open. Luke walked down the corridor, conscious, so conscious, of Aurelie by his side. The whisper of her dress against her bare legs, the citrusy scent of her, the way each breath she took made her chest rise and fall.

She stopped in front of the door to her suite, and he stopped too. She waited, her hand on the door, her eyes wide. Expectant. But he'd promised himself—and her—that he wouldn't touch her until she asked. Until no uncertainty remained.

Standing there, he knew that time had not yet come. Unfortunately for him.

'Goodnight, Aurelie.' He cupped her cheek, just as he had the night before, because despite all his promises he couldn't resist touching her, just a little. Aurelie closed her eyes. Waited. It would be so easy to brush his lips against hers, to deepen the kiss he knew she wanted. But it was too soon, and he'd still seen the shadows in her eyes.

With a supreme act of will he dropped his hand from her face. He smiled—at least he thought he did—and walked down the hall towards his own lonely suite of rooms.

Aurelie stepped inside her empty suite and leaned against the door, her eyes closed.

Damn.

Why hadn't he kissed her? He'd wanted to, she knew that. She'd wanted him to, had willed him to close that small space between them, but instead he'd pulled away.

Maybe you didn't know what you wanted. And until you do, completely, I'm not going to touch you.

His words from yesterday reverberated through her, made her think. Wonder. Was he waiting for her to take the lead? To say she had no more uncertainty, no more fear?

Did she?

No. She was still afraid. She'd been telling Luke the truth when she said she'd never enjoyed sex. If she'd been totally honest, she would have told him she dreaded it. Hated it, and yet used it because at least then she had some control.

And now? She wanted sex—sex with Luke—to be something different. Something more. And that terrified her more than another bout of unenjoyable coupling.

She opened her eyes, paced the room, her mind racing. She wanted this. She wanted Luke. And, just like with her song, with the trust, with the intimacy, she knew she needed to push past the fear. For her sake as much as Luke's.

So...what did that mean, exactly? Right here, right now? She ran her now-damp palms down the sides of her dress.

Brushed her teeth and hair, applied a little perfume. And then before she could overthink it and start to get really nervous, she went in search of Luke.

CHAPTER NINE

LUKE YANKED OPEN his laptop and stared at the spreadsheet he'd left up on the screen. Work was as good an antidote as any to sexual frustration. He didn't have any better ideas, at any rate.

Sighing, he raked his hands through his hair, loosened his tie and stared hard at the screen.

Five minutes later a knock sounded on the door of his suite.

Luke tensed. He wasn't expecting anyone, and his staff would call or text him before disturbing him in his private quarters. So would anyone from the hotel. Another knock, soft, timid. He knew who it was.

'Hello, Aurelie.' He stood in front of the doorway, drinking her in even though he'd seen her just a few minutes ago. Her hair looked even more tousled, her lips soft and full. She'd sunk her teeth into the lower one and he could see the faint bite marks.

'May I come in?'

It reminded him, poignantly, of when he'd first come to her house in Vermont. How he'd asked, how she'd been so reluctant to let him in.

As reluctant as he was now, because he knew how weak he was when it came to this woman. 'All right.' He stepped aside, felt her dress whisper across him as she passed by.

'Do you need something?' he asked as he closed the door. He heard how formal and stiff he sounded, and he could tell she did too.

Her mouth quirked upwards and she took a deep breath. 'Yes. You.'

God help him. Her direct look, eyes wide, lips parted, had pure lust racing right through him. He clenched his fists, unclenched them. Breathed deep. 'I don't think this is a good idea, Aurelie.'

'Funny, I think you've said that before.'

'I know. And it wasn't a good idea then, either.' Hurt flashed across her face and she glanced away. 'It's too soon,' Luke said quietly. 'This is too important to rush things.'

She took a step towards him. 'Maybe it's too important to hold back.'

He shook his head. 'I don't think you're ready.'

'Shouldn't I be the judge of that?'

'Yes, but—' He hesitated. Wondered just why he was fighting this so much. Then he remembered the look on her face when he'd rolled off her before, as if she'd been cast in stone. He'd felt...he'd felt almost like a rapist. Sighing, he raked a hand through his hair and sank onto the sofa. 'Why don't you sit down?'

Gingerly she sat across from him. He thought of how he'd first met her, the cold cynicism in her eyes, the outrageous smile, the constant innuendo. She was so different now, so real and beautiful and vulnerable. He was so afraid of hurting her. Of failing her.

It was a fear, he acknowledged bleakly, that had dogged him for most of his life. Twenty-five years, to be precise, since he'd battered helpless fists against a locked door, begged his mother to let him in. Tried to save her...and failed.

This is your fault, Luke.

He blinked, forced the memory away. He hardly ever

thought of it now, had schooled himself not to. Yet Aurelie's fragile vulnerability brought it all rushing back, made him agonisingly aware of his own responsibility—and weakness.

'It's not as if I'm a virgin,' she said, clearly trying to sound light and playful and not quite achieving it. 'Even if you're acting as if I am.'

'In some ways you are,' Luke answered bluntly. 'If you've never enjoyed sex—'

'I'm what? An enjoyment virgin?' Her eyebrows rose, and he saw a faint remnant of the old mockery there.

'An emotional one, perhaps.'

She sighed. 'Semantics again.'

'I don't know what sex has been to you in the past, but it's not anything I want it to be with me.'

A blush touched her cheeks. 'I know that. I want it to be different.'

'How?'

She swallowed. 'Maybe you should tell me what it's been to you in the past.'

Now he swallowed. Looked away. He was so not used to these kinds of conversations. Honesty and emotional nakedness were two totally different things. 'Well, I suppose it's been an expression of affection.' *Coward.* 'Of…of love.'

They stared at each other, the silence taut with unspoken words, feelings too new and fragile to articulate. 'Did you love the women you've been with before?' Aurelie asked in a low voice.

'I suppose I thought I did. But honestly, I'm not sure.' He raked a hand through his hair. 'It didn't feel like this.'

This. Whatever was between them, whatever they were building. Luke didn't know how strong it was, whether a single breath would knock it all down.

'That's what I want,' Aurelie finally managed, her voice no more than a husky whisper. 'I know we've only known each other a short while and I'm not saying—' She cleared her throat. 'I'm not trying to, you know, jump the gun.'

His mouth twisted wryly. 'Aren't you?'

'Well, not the emotional gun. Physically, maybe.'

He shook his head slowly. 'They go together, Aurelie. That's the only kind of sex I want with you.'

He saw the fear flash in her eyes but she didn't look away. 'That's what I want, Luke. That's what I want with you.'

And he wanted to believe her. Yet still he hesitated; they'd only known each other, really, for a handful of days. Intense days, yes, amazing days. But still just days.

'Please,' she whispered, her voice low and smoky, and he felt his resistance start to crumble. Not that there had really been much to begin with. He was honest enough—hell, yes, he had to be—to know that any resistance he'd given had been token, merely a show. He wanted this too.

'Anything that happens between us,' he said, his tone turning almost severe, 'happens at a pace I control.'

She stilled for just a second, then gave him a small smile. 'Yes, boss.'

'And if I think it isn't…it isn't working, then we stop. *I* stop. Got that?'

'Got it.'

Hell. He hadn't exactly set the mood, had he? Yet he wanted her to know he wasn't going to rush things, take advantage. In this crucial moment, he wanted her to trust him. He wanted to trust himself.

He swallowed, felt her gaze, wide-eyed and expectant, on him. He could not think of a single thing to say.

A tiny smile hovered around Aurelie's mouth and her eyes lightened with mischief. 'So what now?'

'Hell if I know.'

And then she laughed, a joyous bubble of sound, and he

laughed too, and he felt them both relax. Maybe it would be okay after all. Maybe it would even be wonderful.

He stood up, held his hand out to her. She took it instantly, instinctively, trusting him already. 'Come on.'

He led her to the bedroom in the back of the suite, two walls of windows overlooking the inky surface of Marina Bay. Aurelie only had eyes for the bed. It was big, wide and piled with pillows in different shades of blue silk. She turned to him and licked her lips, a question in her eyes.

'Let's just relax.' He kicked off his shoes, took off his tie and stretched out on the bed. Aurelie sat on its edge and took off her boots. Gingerly she scooted up next to him, lay her head back on the pillows. Luke laughed softly. 'You look like you're on an examining table.'

'I feel a bit like that too.'

'We're not rushing this, you know.'

'I almost wish you would.'

'Oh?' He arched an eyebrow. 'You think you'd enjoy that?'

Now she laughed, the soft sound trembling on the air. 'Probably not.'

Gently he traced the winged arches of her eyebrows, the curve of her cheek. Her eyes fluttered closed and he let himself explore the graceful contours of her face with his fingertips: the straight line of her nose, the fullness of her lips. 'Tell me,' he asked after a moment, 'what your favourite room is in your house in Vermont.'

'What?' Her eyes opened and she stared at him in surprise. Luke smiled and gently closed them again with his fingertips.

'Your favourite room,' he repeated and continued to stroke her face with whisper-light touches. He felt her relax, just a little.

'The kitchen, I suppose. I always remember my grandmother there.'

'She liked to bake?'

'Yes—'

'And you helped her that summer?'

Her eyes opened again, clear with astonishment. 'Yes—' Gently he nudged them closed once more. She relaxed back into the pillows again. 'I always liked helping her with things,' she said after a moment. 'I suppose because she always liked me to help.'

'You must miss her,' Luke said quietly, and she gave a little nod.

'You must miss your mother,' she said, her voice hardly more than a whisper, and for a second his fingers stilled on her face. He hadn't expected her to say *that*. She opened her eyes, gave him a small smile. 'This honesty thing? You told me it went both ways.'

'Yes.' But he really didn't want to talk about his mother.

'Do you miss her?'

'Yes.' He swallowed, felt his throat thicken. 'Every day.' Gently he traced the outline of her parted lips with his fingers and then slowly, deliberately, dropped his finger to her chin. Rested it there for a moment. 'You know, the first time I met you I knew the truth of you from your chin.'

'My chin?'

'It quivers when you're upset.'

She laughed softly. 'No one's ever told me that before.'

'Maybe no one's ever noticed.' He lowered his head and pressed a kiss to the point of her chin. He felt her still, hold her breath. *Wait.* He lifted his head and smiled. 'I like it.'

'I'm glad.'

He touched her chin once more with his fingertip, and then trailed it slowly down the curve of her neck, rested it in the sweet little hollow of her throat. Stroked. He heard her breath hitch and she shifted on the bed. Luke felt the impatient stirring of his own desire. He'd told her they'd go slowly, and he meant it. Even if it was a rather painful process for him. 'Your skin is so soft. I thought that the first time I met you too.'

'You didn't.'

'I did. I was attracted to you from the moment you opened your eyes. Why do you think I was so ticked off?'

She let out a shuddery little laugh as he continued to stroke that little hollow. 'Because I was passed out and running late, I thought.'

'That was just my cover.' He let his finger trace a gentle line from the hollow of her throat down to the vee between her breasts. And he rested it there, the sides of her breasts softly brushing his finger, and waited.

Her cheeks were faintly flushed now, and her eyes had fluttered closed. He heard her breath rise and fall with a slight shudder and he felt a deep surge of satisfaction. She wanted this. She wanted him. He trailed his finger back up to that hollow, and she opened her eyes.

'This is going to take forever.'

He laughed softly. 'Not forever, I hope. That would kill me.' He let his finger trail back down, brushed the soft sides of her breasts this time, and felt her shiver. 'But long enough.' He pressed his lips to the hollow of her throat and then he slid his palm down to cup the soft fullness of her breast. She tensed for a second and then relaxed into the caress with a soft sigh.

Luke felt a powerful surge of protectiveness. He wanted to do this right. But it was killing him to go so slowly, to take the time he knew she needed. He flicked his thumb over the peak of her nipple and heard her indrawn breath, then another sigh. He smiled and moved his hand lower, onto the taut muscles of her tummy.

She opened her eyes, gazed up at him. 'You're being incredibly patient.'

'It's worth it.'

'You don't know that.'

'I know.' He slid his hand lower, down to her bare knee, and rested it there. Watched her eyes widen in expectation, maybe alarm. He stroked the back of her knee, down to the slender bones of her ankle, and then back up again. A little further up, so his fingers brushed the tender, silky skin of her inner thigh and then down again to the safety of that knee.

She let out a little laugh. 'You're torturing me.'

'Am I?' With his other hand he touched her cheek, the fullness of her lower lip, her chin, the hollow of her throat. Saw her eyes go hazy and dark with desire. She reached her hands up and tangled them in his hair, drew him closer.

'Kiss me,' she commanded, her voice husky, and Luke obliged.

He brushed his lips across her once, twice, and then went deep, tasting her as she tasted him. His hand tightened instinctively on her knee, slid upwards. She parted her legs and he felt her hands go to the buttons of his shirt.

'Too many clothes,' she mumbled against his mouth, and in a couple of quick shrugs—and a few buttons popping—he was free of his shirt, the garment tossed to the floor.

'How about your dress?'

She swallowed, nodded, and he slid the skinny straps from her shoulders. One quick, sinuous tug on the zip on the back and she shimmied out of the dress, kicking it away from her ankles.

Luke gazed at her. He'd seen her in her underwear before, of course, but he still loved to look at her. He let his gaze travel back up to her face, those wide, stormy eyes. 'Okay?' he asked quietly, and she nodded.

Still he waited. She nodded towards his trousers. 'Maybe you should deal with those.'

'Maybe you should.'

She arched her eyebrows, then smiled and nodded. Luke bit down on a groan as her fingers brushed his arousal. She fumbled a bit with the belt and zip, which made it all the more of an exquisite torture. Then she slid his trousers off his hips, and he kicked them the rest of the way. All they were wearing was their underwear, and it felt like way too much clothing to him. He smoothed his hand from her shoulder to her hip, revelling in the feel of her satiny skin. She shivered under his touch and he moved his hand upwards again, cupped her breast and smiled as she arched into his hand.

He kissed her again, deeply, and felt her respond, her arms coming around him, one leg twining with his. He moved his hand lower, across her tummy to the juncture of her thighs. Waited there, feeling her warmth, until she parted her legs and he slipped his fingers inside her underwear, felt her tense and then will herself to relax, arching her hips upwards as his fingers explored and teased her.

He felt his control slipping a notch as her own hand skimmed his erection and their tongues tangled, heard her breathing hitch—or was it his? He was so, so ready for this, and she *felt* ready—

He pressed another kiss to her throat, willed his heart to stop racing. 'Okay?' he muttered against her neck, and felt her nod. He slid her underwear off, kicked off his own boxer shorts. And then he was poised between her thighs, aching with need for her, their bodies pressed slickly together, all of him anticipating and straining towards this—

He looked down and saw she'd gone still, actually *rigid*, with her eyes scrunched tightly shut.

Damn.

It took all, absolutely all of Luke's self-control to stop. He took a deep, shuddering breath and rolled off her onto his back. Stared at the ceiling and felt his heart wrench inside him when he heard Aurelie let out a tiny hiccup of a sob. *What had gone wrong?* And how had he let this happen—again?

'I'm sorry,' she finally whispered into the silence.

'No. Don't be.' He was still staring at the ceiling, still feeling that scalding rush of shame and guilt. He was also feeling incredibly, painfully aroused. 'Let me just take a shower,' he muttered and, rolling off the bed, he headed towards the bathroom.

Aurelie lay on the bed and listened to Luke turn on the shower. She blinked hard and tried not to cry. *What had gone wrong?*

She honestly didn't know. One second she'd been lost in Luke's little touches, aching for his deeper caress—and the next? She'd felt the heavy weight on top of her and his breath in her ear and suddenly, painfully been reminded of the first time with Pete.

Let me...

She blinked hard again, forced the memories back. She did not want to think of them now, to bring them into this moment, this bed.

Drawing a deep breath, she reached for her scattered clothes. She didn't even remember Luke unclasping her bra, but he must have done. It was lying on the floor. She dressed quickly, furtively, afraid Luke would come out of the bathroom—and then what? Was he angry? Frustrated, no doubt, in more ways than one. And knowing Luke—which she did now, she realised—he'd want answers. Answers she didn't want to give, because she knew they wouldn't reflect well on herself.

Sighing, she sat back down on the bed and waited.

A few minutes later Luke emerged from the bathroom, a towel around his hips. Aurelie swallowed dryly at the sight of his chest, broad, browned and shimmering with droplets of water. Just a few minutes ago she'd had the power to touch it at her leisure, had felt that hard, muscular body pressed against hers. Just the memory caused a pulse of desire low in her belly. *How* had it all gone wrong? Could memories really have that much power?

Luke reached for a T-shirt and dropped his towel, oblivious to his own nakedness. Aurelie was not. She swallowed again, felt her heart start to thud. He slipped on a pair of boxers and then sat on the edge of the bed. She tensed, waited.

He smiled wryly, his eyes dark, his hair damp and spiky. She wanted to comb it with her fingers, to feel its damp softness. She folded her hands together in her lap.

'I guess you realise we need to talk.' She nodded, and Luke sighed. 'I'm sorry for the way things happened.'

'Don't be.' It hurt to squeeze those two words out, for her throat had got absurdly tight. 'It's not your fault.'

'It's not yours, either.' She didn't answer, and Luke reached over and placed his hand over her tightly clasped ones, his thumb stroking her fingers. 'Tell me what happened to you, Aurelie.'

'Nothing happened.' She shook her head, impatient with the way he was making her a victim. She'd never wanted pity. She'd made all her choices willingly. She *had*.

'Why, then,' Luke asked evenly, 'did you freeze up at a rather crucial point? Everything was going well, wasn't it?'

She let out a little choked sound, half-laugh, half-sob. 'Very well.'

'And then?'

'I don't know. I just—' She moistened her lips, forced herself to continue. 'I just froze up, like you said. To be honest, you're the only one who's ever noticed.'

'Then you haven't had very considerate lovers.'

'No.'

Luke sighed and squeezed her hand. 'I appreciate that I

may not have earned enough of your trust to tell me what happened to you, because something did. Some experience has made you fear sex and, until I know what it is, I can't help you. And,' he added, a wry note entering his voice, 'I can't make love to you, which is a shame.'

Aurelie lifted her gaze to his. 'We could try again—'

'No.' Luke spoke with such flat finality that she recoiled. 'I don't think you realise,' he added more quietly, 'how it makes me feel to see you beneath me, looking like you're bracing yourself for some kind of torture.'

She blinked, felt the hot wetness of tears behind her lids. She hadn't thought of that. She'd only thought of herself, and how disappointing she must be to him. 'I'm sorry,' she whispered.

'I don't want your apologies. I just want your honesty. But I can wait.'

She sniffed. Loudly. 'So what now?'

'How about we go to sleep?'

Hope stirred inside her, a tiny, fragile bud emerging amidst the mire of desolation. 'Here? Together?'

'That's the idea.' And then, gently, perhaps even lovingly, he pulled her into his arms so her cheek rested against that wonderfully hard chest. She felt the reassuring thud of his heart and closed her eyes. 'I'm a patient man, Aurelie.'

She smiled against his chest, even though the tears still felt all too close. 'That's good to know.'

Yet as she snuggled against him beneath the covers, his arms securely around her, she wondered if she was the impatient one. She'd changed and grown so much over the last few days, but she wanted more. She wanted to be different in *every* way, and especially in this one. Yet with this—this crucial intimacy—she didn't know how to change, or even if she could.

CHAPTER TEN

MORNING SUNLIGHT SPILLED across the bed, created pools of warmth amidst the nest of covers. Aurelie rose on one elbow and stared down at the sleeping form of the man she loved.

Yes, loved. She'd been skirting around that obvious truth for days now, because it was too scary and even impossible to grasp. How could she love a man she'd known for such a short time? And why would she, when she knew what happened when you gave your heart away? You lost not just the heart you'd freely given, but your soul as well. Your very self.

She knew Luke was different. She knew it bone-deep, *soul*-deep, and yet that knowledge didn't stay the tattoo of fear beating through her blood. The memory of how absolutely wrecked she'd been when Pete had finally ended it, and how she'd realised she had nothing, *was* nothing but a shell, remained with her. Infected her with doubt.

She didn't doubt that Luke was different; she feared that she wasn't. Even now a sly, insidious voice mocked that she hadn't changed at all, not in the way that mattered most. She'd give herself to him, body and heart and soul, and he would take it and use it and there would be nothing left. She'd be nothing.

And yet, despite that consuming fear, she still felt that baby's breath of hope, and Luke's steady presence, his arms cradling her all night long, had fanned it into something strong and good.

She wanted to take a chance again. With Luke, and with herself.

He opened his eyes.

'Good morning.' His voice was low and husky, and its warmth flooded through her. She smiled.

'Good morning.'

He shifted so she was cradled once more by his arm, and she rested her head on his shoulder, breathed in the warm, woodsy scent of him. Idly he ran a few strands of hair through his fingers. 'Sleep well?'

'Better than I can ever remember.'

He pulled her just a little bit closer, that primal part of him clearly satisfied. 'Good.'

Aurelie took a breath. And another, because this was hard. *So* hard, and as she took another breath she knew she was already starting to hyperventilate. She let it out slowly, a long, breathy sigh, and Luke's hand stilled on her hair. He was waiting.

'I want to tell you some things,' she began, and deliberately he began stroking her hair again, his fingers sifting through the strands.

'Okay.'

'I think I'm ready to…to do that.' He didn't answer, just kept stroking, and Aurelie closed her eyes. 'Not that it's that big a story. I mean, if you're expecting me to tell you something horrible to explain…well, to explain my behaviour, it wasn't like that.'

'You don't need to make any judgements, Aurelie. I won't.'

She felt her eyes scrunch shut, as if she could block out the truth she was about to tell. 'You might.'

'No.'

'I told you I haven't been a Girl Scout. Some of those tab-

loid stories—a lot of them—are true.' She spoke almost defiantly now, daring him to be shocked. Disgusted.

'I know that,' Luke answered steadily. He was so steady,
even when she was doing her best to push him away and pull
him closer both at the same time.

'I have to go back to the beginning.'

'I told you I am a patient man.'

'I know.' And now all there was left to do was begin. At
the beginning. 'You remember I told you I was discovered
at that karaoke night in Kansas?'

'Yes.'

'The man who discovered me was named Pete.'

'Pete Myers,' Luke clarified, and Aurelie realised that he'd
heard of him, of *course* he'd heard of him. Pete was famous.
He'd managed several major bands, had judged a couple of
TV talent shows. He was practically a household name.

'Right,' she said, and continued. 'Well, Pete was amazing
back then. He came up to me, told me he could make me a
star. He took my mom and me to dinner, told us his whole
plan. How I'd become Aurelie.'

'So he was the one behind your image.' Luke spoke tone-
lessly, but Aurelie still felt the censure. She stiffened.

'I went along with it. Innocent siren, those were his
words.'

'You were only fifteen.'

'Almost sixteen. And I thought it all sounded incredibly
cool.' She sighed, hating that already she was having to explain, to justify. Luke's arm tightened around her.

'I'm sorry. Continue.'

'Those first few months were a whirlwind. Pete took us
all over, to LA, New York, Nashville. I met with agents and
songwriters and publicity people and, before I knew what
was happening, I was recording and releasing a single, and
it was huge. I felt like I was at the centre of a storm.'

'What about your mother?'

'She disappeared a couple of months after Pete discovered me. I think she realised people didn't really want her around, that she was just getting in the way. When she left, Pete offered to have me stay with him. I was still a minor, and he had to make some kind of legal guardian arrangement with my grandmother—' She stopped then, because her throat had become so tight. That had been the last time she'd seen her grandmother alive. She'd given her the guitar, begged her to stay the same. And she hadn't.

'Anyway,' she continued, trying desperately for briskness, 'Pete was great about it all. He gave me my own floor in his house, treated me like—' the word stuck in her throat '—a daughter. At least, he felt like a father to me. The dad I'd never had. He gave me a lot of good advice in the early days, how not to take any of the criticism to heart, how to stay sane amidst all the craziness. He even remembered my birthday—he got me a cake for my seventeenth.'

'A paragon,' Luke said flatly, and she squirmed in his arms to face him.

'I told you not to make judgements.'

'I'm not. I'm just wondering where this is going.'

'I'll tell you.' She took another breath, let it out slowly. 'I'd been living with Pete for a little over a year. He'd seen me through some tough times—my grandmother dying, being diagnosed with diabetes. He was the one who found me, you know. I'd passed out in the bathroom, and he took me to ER. Stayed with me the whole time, made sure I got the proper treatment and counselling once I was diagnosed.' She felt Luke's tension; his shoulder was iron-hard under her cheek. 'I'm telling you all this just to...to explain the relationship. How close we were.'

'I get it.' His tone was even, expressionless, and yet Aurelie sensed the darkness underneath. And she hadn't really told him anything yet.

'So fast forward to my eighteenth birthday. He took me out to dinner at The Ivy, told me how happy he was that I'd made it, how much he cared about me.' She paused, tried to choose her words carefully. She needed the right ones. 'I look back on that as one of the happiest nights of my life.' Before it had all changed.

She fell silent, the only sound in the bedroom the draw and sigh of their breathing. 'And then?' Luke asked eventually. 'What happened?'

'Pete took me home. I went to bed. I was just changing into my pyjamas when he…he came into the room.' He hadn't, she remembered now, asked to come in. Not like Luke. She still remembered that ripple of shocked confusion at seeing Pete standing in the doorway. Staring at her.

'And?' Luke asked very quietly. Aurelie realised she'd stopped speaking. She was just remembering, and she hated it.

'He told me he loved me. He'd always loved me, and then he…he kissed me.'

'Not,' Luke said quietly, 'like a dad.'

'No. Not like a dad.' She still remembered the shocking feel of his mouth on hers, wet and insistent. The way his hands had roved over her body, with a kind of tentative urgency. He'd been crying a little bit, and he kept begging her. *Let me,* he had whispered over and over again, and she had.

'What did you do?' Luke asked. He was still stroking her hair, still holding her. Aurelie blinked back the memories.

'I let him.'

'Let him?'

'He kept saying that. *Let me.* And I did, because…well, because I didn't want to lose him. He was the most important person in my life at that point, the only person in my life. And, looking back, I can see how I got it wrong. He never wanted to be my dad. I was the one who wanted that.'

Luke's hands had stilled. 'So he...he kissed you?'

'We had sex,' Aurelie said flatly. 'That night. It was, if you can believe it, my first time. That whole innocent siren thing? It was pretty much true.'

Luke swallowed, said nothing. 'I didn't enjoy it,' she continued. She felt weirdly emotionless now, as if none of it mattered. 'I hated it. It felt...well, it felt gross, to be honest. But I knew it was what he wanted and so I made myself want it too.'

'And what happened then? After?'

She shrugged. 'We started dating.'

'Dating?'

'A relationship. Whatever. I was already living with him, so—'

'Are you telling me,' Luke asked, and his voice shook slightly, 'that Pete Myers was your serious relationship? The one that lasted three years?'

'Yes—'

'God, Aurelie.' He sank back onto the pillows and when she risked a look at his face she saw he looked shocked. Winded, as if she'd just punched him. Maybe she had.

'I thought you kind of knew where this was going.'

'Well, when you started talking about Myers, I figured he'd...he'd taken advantage of you somehow. But you'd said you weren't abused or raped—'

'I wasn't.' She stared at him in surprise. 'I told you, he asked.' *Let me.* 'And I said yes.'

Luke stared at her. He still looked dazed. 'You remember when we talked about semantics?'

'Yes—'

'Yeah. That.'

She shook her head. 'I wasn't a victim. If I'd told him to leave, he would have.'

'You think so?'

'I know it. Luke, you weren't there. You didn't see how... how pathetic he looked. I felt sorry for him.' Almost.

'Yeah, I'm sure he could look pathetic when he wanted to. He's also one of the richest, most powerful men in the music world, Aurelie. You don't think he might have been taking advantage of you?'

'Maybe,' she allowed, 'but I allowed it to happen.'

'For three years.'

'It was a *relationship*.' She didn't like the tone Luke took, as if she'd been used. Abused. A victim.

'A secret relationship. I've never seen this mentioned in the press.'

'Pete didn't want the tabloids to trash us. He was being protective—'

'Very thoughtful of him.'

'Don't,' she said furiously. 'Don't make this about me being used by him. I was *not* a victim.'

Luke just gazed at her. 'Go on,' he finally said quietly. 'Tell me what happened.'

'When?'

'How did it end?'

'He ended it. He said it wasn't working, that I was too clingy.'

'Too clingy.'

'Yes. And I was, I can see that now. The fame had started to get to me, and I felt like Pete was the only person who knew who I really was. My mom was still out of the picture, my grandma was dead, and I'd never stayed in one place long enough to get to know anyone.'

'So,' Luke said slowly, 'he was all you had.'

'It felt that way. But he started losing interest and my

music started slipping, the media noticed, and when he finally ended it—' She took a breath, plunged. 'I went off the deep end.'

'You weren't,' Luke said, and she almost heard a sad smile in his voice, 'a Girl Scout.'

'No. I pretty much did what the press said I did. I drank, I did drugs, I partied hard and slept around, and my career tanked.' She swallowed, sniffed. 'So there you have it.'

Luke said nothing, and Aurelie felt condemnation in his silence. She'd done so many things she wasn't proud of, the first one being that she'd given in to Pete that first night. That she'd been so clingy and needy and starved of love, she'd taken what she could get. And then when he'd decided he didn't want her any more, she'd spun out of control because she'd felt so horribly empty.

And she was so afraid of that happening again.

'Which part of all that,' Luke finally asked, 'did you not want to tell me?'

She let out a wobbly laugh, surprised by the question. 'All of it.'

'But which part in particular?' He shifted so he was facing her, his gaze intent, his eyes blazing. 'The part at the end? About how you went off the deep end? How you partied and slept around and lost yourself?'

She squirmed under that gaze, those pointed, knowing questions. 'Yes, basically.' *Lost yourself.* That was exactly what had happened, yet even now she couldn't admit as much to Luke. Admit that she was afraid of it happening again, and worse this time. She'd finally found herself again, thanks to Luke. But what if she lost herself once more because she couldn't handle being in a relationship? Being hurt?

What if he grew tired of her like Pete had, like the whole *world* had?

'And what about sex?' he asked quietly. 'Enjoying it? Why do you think you don't?'

She swallowed, wished he didn't have to be quite so blunt. 'I suppose because of my experience with Pete. I was never attracted to him, and being with him like that for so long… it just killed that part of me.'

'And when I'm with you? And you freeze? Why do you think that is?'

'I don't know.' She felt herself getting angry again. She hated him asking so many terrible questions, stripping her so horribly bare. 'I suppose I remember that first time. It was awful, okay?' Tears sprang to her eyes and she turned her face away from him. *'Awful.* I couldn't breathe. He was so heavy. And it…hurt.' She gasped the last word out, tears pooling in her eyes. If she blinked they would fall, and she couldn't have that. If she let those first tears out, too many more would follow, and she was afraid she would never stop crying.

'What about with other men?' Luke asked quietly.

Aurelie sniffed, her face still averted, her voice clogged with all those mortifying tears. 'They were all pretty much the same. They only wanted one thing from me, and I knew that. I was a trophy. I got it, and I used it because—' She stopped, and Luke finished for her, his voice so soft and sad.

'Because it was better than being used.'

She said nothing. Words were beyond her. She wished she'd never told him, desperately wished she hadn't opened up this Pandora's box of tawdry memories. 'Don't judge me,' she finally whispered, a plea, and Luke shook his head.

'I'm not judging you. Not at all.'

He sounded so weary, so resigned, that Aurelie felt her spirits plummet, and they were already pretty low. He was disgusted by her. Of course he was. How could he not be, after all the things she'd told him? She'd known this would happen. She'd been expecting it. She slipped away from him, rolled out of bed and hunted for her dress.

'I should go back to my room.'

'Why?'

'We're going to Hong Kong today, right? I need to shower and get dressed.' She didn't look at him as she slipped her dress on, tugged on her boots. Her hair was a disaster, but all she needed to do was walk down the hall.

'We're not finished here, Aurelie.'

'I'm finished.'

'You're scared.'

Hell, yes. She glanced up at him, hands on her hips. 'Oh, you think so? Of what?'

'A lot of things, I suspect.'

Luke sounded so calm, so relaxed, and here she was feeling like a butterfly pinned to a board. Unable to protect or hide herself, just out there for his relentless examination. 'Well, I'm not scared,' she snapped. 'But I don't particularly like talking about all that, and since we have a full day I'd like to get on with it. That all right by you?' She spoke in a sneering drawl, the kind of voice she'd used so many times before. The kind of voice she hadn't used with Luke since they'd started on their second chance.

Well, so much for that.

'It's all right by me,' he said quietly and, without another word, Aurelie whirled around and stalked out of his bedroom.

Luke lay on the bed and stared at the ceiling, too dazed to do anything but try and process what Aurelie had told him. *Pete Myers.* A man who had to have been at least fifty when he'd first started with Aurelie. A man who had abused her affection, used her body and her trust. And Aurelie didn't see it that way.

She saw it as a *relationship.* Hell, no.

Sighing, he ran his hands through his hair, pressed his fists into his eyes. He had no idea what to do. He was still so afraid of failing her. Failing her like he had last night, when he'd gone about it completely wrong. He'd been trying to ease Aurelie into love-making gently, sweetly, but he'd been the one in control. Hell, he'd told her that before they even started. *Anything that happens between us, happens at a pace I control... Got that?*

He winced at the memory. He'd thought it would help her, to know they would go slowly, but now he saw how it must have accomplished the opposite. He'd been just another man controlling her, using her body. Luke swore aloud.

He saw now that Aurelie needed to feel in control. To *be* in control. That was, he suspected, why she insisted on believing Pete hadn't taken advantage of her, that it had been a willing, committed relationship—because then it was something she could control.

And last night, in an utterly misguided attempt to help her, he'd quite literally taken all the control away from her. Groaning aloud, Luke dropped his fists from his eyes and stared at the ceiling once more. It was time, he knew, for a third chance. Time to earn her trust once more.

By the time he'd showered and dressed, eaten and answered emails, he was near to running late. He'd knocked on the door of Aurelie's room but there had been no answer and he felt a flicker of foreboding. Was she trying to avoid him? Well, that could only last so long.

His mouth firming into a determined line, he headed downstairs.

Aurelie was waiting in the lobby, dressed in a mint-green shift dress, her hair tucked behind her ears, her arms folded. She was fidgeting and she didn't meet his gaze as he came towards her. Clearly now was not the time to have some kind

of emotional discussion, and maybe he needed the time—
the break—too.

'All ready?' he asked lightly, and she nodded tensely, her
gaze fixed somewhere around his shoulder.

They didn't speak in the limo on the way to the airport, or
as they boarded the jet that would take them to Hong Kong.
Luke pulled out some papers, thinking to work, but then he
decided he wasn't that patient after all.

'Aurelie.' She turned towards him, still not meeting his
eyes. 'You're doing a pretty good job of avoiding me even
though I'm right here.'

She lowered her head so her hair fell forward in front of
her face. 'I don't know what to say to you.'

'Maybe you could tell me what you're thinking.'

'That.'

He sighed and slipped his papers back into a manila folder.
'What else?'

She shook her head, bit her lip. Luke just waited. 'I'm
thinking I wish I hadn't told you everything I did this morning.'

'Why not?'

'Because…' she lifted her gaze to his, and he saw the
storm in her eyes '…because you think of me differently
now, and I can't stand that—'

'I wouldn't say differently.'

'What, then?'

'More sympathetically—'

She shook her head, the movement violent. 'I don't want
your pity.'

'It's not pity to be able to understand you—'

'I am not some kind of psychological *specimen*—'

'I never said you were.' Luke felt his temper start to fray.
He would *never* say the right thing. 'Aurelie, you're going

to tank us right here and now if you keep fighting me like this. I'm just trying to make this *work*.'

She hunched her shoulders, her chin tucked low. 'Maybe it can't.'

'Is that what you want?' he asked evenly, and she didn't answer for a moment. Fear lurched inside him. Already he couldn't stand the thought of losing her.

'No,' she finally said, her voice so low he had to strain to hear her. She sighed and rested her head against the seat, her eyes closed. 'Look, I know I'm making a mess of this. But I told you in the beginning that I don't know how to let my guard down—'

'You've already let your guard down. Now you're just desperately trying to assemble it again.'

She let out a soft huff of laughter and lifted her wry, slate-blue gaze to his. 'That's not working, is it?'

'No. And I don't want it to work.' He didn't know what the future held, and he still felt that old fear, but he did know he wanted to keep trying. He hoped she did too.

She glanced away. 'I don't, either.' She nibbled her lip, and he thought about reaching out to touch her. Comfort her. He stayed where he was. The physical aspect of their relationship would be dealt with later. He hoped. 'I'm scared,' she said softly, still not looking at him. 'I'm so scared of losing myself again. Of losing control, of not being able to change.'

'Every relationship contains an element of loss of control, but that doesn't mean you have to lose yourself completely. A relationship should make you better, stronger. More of yourself rather than less.' He smiled wryly. 'Or so all the chat shows and women's magazines tell me.'

She arched her eyebrows. 'You watch chat shows and read women's magazines?'

'All the time.'

She laughed, and he smiled. Miraculously, it felt okay again. 'Sorry,' she said softly, and he shook his head.

'This isn't about sorry.'

'What is it about, then?'

'Trust. You're still learning to trust me. I'm still trying to earn it.'

'You have earned it, Luke.'

He didn't feel as if he had. He'd let her down too many times already. *You're always letting people down. The people that matter most.*

That sly inner voice mocked him, reminded him of his failures. The locked door, his mother's silence. His own. He was still living in the long shadow of that moment, and he hated it. So much of Aurelie's life had been defined by one man's selfish actions. Had his life been similarly defined? Destroyed?

Could he rebuild it again, now, with her?

'We land in an hour,' he said, trying to smile, and felt his heart lift and lighten when Aurelie smiled back.

Aurelie had never been to Hong Kong before, and even though she'd seen photos she wasn't prepared for the sheer scale of the city, the skyscrapers clustered so close together, right to the edge of Victoria Harbour, piercing the sky.

She still felt raw from the conversation with Luke on the plane. This honesty was a killer. And when she caught him looking at her with a kind of sorrowful compassion, she froze inside. Part of her ached for the understanding he offered, and yet another part scrambled away in self-protection. Did she really want to be understood, all the dark parts of herself brought to glaring light?

He knew the worst, at least in broad strokes. He knew that she'd gone into a relationship—an awful, unhealthy relationship—out of pathetic loneliness and fear, and he understood, if not in the tawdry particulars, how she'd reacted when it had ended. The many, many bad choices she'd made.

And he's still here.

The voice that whispered inside her wasn't sly or cynical for once. It was the still, small voice of hope, of truth. *He's still here.*

She'd told him he'd earned her trust, but she wasn't acting as if he had. She wasn't, Aurelie knew, acting as if she trusted him at all.

Could she act that way? Deliberately, a decision? Was change not so much a wishing or a hoped-for thing, but a choice? An act of will?

'You ready?' Luke called back to her and, nodding, Aurelie stepped from the plane.

The day passed in an exhausting blur of meetings with various important people, touring the city. As if from a distance, Aurelie took in the Peak, the Jade Market, the Giant Buddha. She chatted and smiled and laughed and listened, yet all the while she felt as if she were somewhere else, thinking something else.

Can I do this? Can I act differently with Luke, even when every part of me struggles to protect myself?

After a lengthy dinner with many speeches and toasts, they boarded a yacht for a pleasure cruise in the harbour. Aurelie watched Luke circulate through the guests, and realised with a pang that he looked more relaxed than when she'd seen him in New York or Manila. He looked happy.

Acting differently was a *choice.* An act of will. It had to be. Deliberately she walked across the deck to join him. He stopped his conversation to smile at her briefly, then resumed describing his plan to incorporate more local artists and artisans in the Hong Kong store. He spoke with authority, with a kind of restrained pride, that made Aurelie's heart swell.

She loved this man. She was terrified, but she loved him.

A few minutes later they'd been left alone, and Luke placed his hand on the small of her back as he guided her to the railing. 'Look.'

She looked towards the shore, and saw that the skyscrapers were shimmering with lights.

'It's the Symphony of Lights. It comes on every night at eight o'clock.'

'Amazing.' And it was amazing, to be standing here with this wonderful man, the air warm and sultry, the sky lighting up all around them. She turned to smile at him, felt the smile all the way through her soul. And Luke must have felt it too, must have seen it, because he drew her softly towards him and brushed his lips against hers. A promise. A promise Aurelie intended to keep.

They rode home from the party in a limo, their thighs brushing, the silence between them both comfortable and expectant. Aurelie followed Luke into the lift, up to the top floor where they had separate suites. She stopped at his door, and he looked at her, eyebrows raised.

Aurelie felt her heart beat hard, her mouth dry. She lifted her chin. 'I want to come in.'

Luke rested his keycard in the palm of his hand, gazed at her seriously. She stared steadily back. *This was a choice.* 'We don't have to rush things, Aurelie.'

'I'm not rushing things.'

He gazed evenly at her, assessing, understanding. Then he nodded. 'All right. But I have one condition.' He unlocked the door and opened it, and Aurelie followed him in, her heart thudding even harder now.

'And that is?' she asked when he hadn't said anything, just shed his jacket and loosened his tie.

Luke turned to her, his eyes glinting, everything about him sexy and rumpled and gorgeous. 'My condition,' he said, taking off his tie, 'is that we do this on your terms.'

CHAPTER ELEVEN

'WE...WHAT?' AURELIE blinked. '*My* terms?'

Luke nodded, his eyes still glinting, his mouth curving in a smile even though she could sense how serious he was. 'Yes. Your terms. I've been thinking a lot about what happened before and I realise I handled everything wrong—'

'Everything, Luke? I think that might be a slight exaggeration.'

'Slight,' he agreed wryly. 'But I was the one in control, wasn't I? I told you that from the beginning. I said I'd set the pace, and I'd call it off if I didn't think it was working.'

Warily she nodded, folded her arms. She wasn't sure where he was going with this. 'Your terms.'

'Yes, and they weren't the right ones.'

'Why not?'

'From what you've told me, and from what I know about you, control is kind of a big thing.'

She prickled, resisting any kind of analysis. 'You think?'

'I do.'

She let out a slow breath, forced herself to relax even though every instinct had her reaching for armour, for the defence of mockery. 'Well, who doesn't want to be in control, really?'

'No one, I suppose,' Luke agreed quietly, 'and especially not someone who had no choice about where to live or when to move or what school to go to. Or even, really, how famous she wanted to be.'

She felt that first, sudden sting of tears and shook her head. 'Don't.'

'Why not?'

'Because I can't stand being pitied, I told you that—'

'I know, and that's a kind of keeping control, isn't it? You keep insisting that everything was your choice because if it wasn't you're a victim and you can't stand that thought.'

No, she couldn't, and even though she'd never articulated it to herself, Luke had. Luke understood her—far too well. She managed a very shaky smile. 'These are so not my terms.'

'I know, Aurelie. I'm breaking my own rules here, but I need to say this.' He took a step closer to her. 'As soon as the clothes start coming off, you can call all the shots.'

She let out a wobbly laugh. 'Promise?'

'Cross my heart.' He took another step towards her, reached for her hands. 'What you had with Pete Myers was *not* a relationship.'

Her hands tensed underneath his. 'It felt like one.'

'No, it didn't. You have nothing to compare it with, so trust me on this, okay?'

Trust. It always came down to trust. She blinked, swallowed. Willed herself to keep her hands in his, not to pull away. For once. 'So what was it, then?'

'Abuse.'

'No.' Now she did pull her hands away from his. She turned away from him, wrapping her arms around herself as if she were cold. She was cold, but on the inside.

'How old was he when he first kissed you?'

'Why does the age difference even matter? Plenty of people—'

'Fifty?'

'Forty-nine,' she snapped. 'That doesn't *matter*.'

'It doesn't always matter,' Luke agreed quietly. 'But in this case, when you were young, impressionable, utterly dependent on him—he must have known you thought of him like a father, Aurelie. And he knew you had no one else in the world. He took advantage of you—'

'That doesn't make it *abuse*.'

'I won't argue about semantics. What I'm trying to say is you can't judge any other relationship by what happened with that man. It wasn't healthy or right. Whether you acknowledge it or not, he took all the control away from you, even if you think you let him. Your responses weren't normal because the situation wasn't normal or fair. At all.'

She didn't answer because she had no words. She realised, belatedly, she was shivering. Uncontrollably. She hated everything Luke was saying. She hated it because she knew, in a deep and dark part of herself, that he was right.

And she couldn't stand that thought. Couldn't bear to think so much of her life had been wasted, *used*. She'd been such a pathetic victim.

'I'm sorry,' Luke said softly. 'I'm sorry for what happened to you.'

She didn't answer. Words wouldn't come. She blinked hard and turned around. 'So my terms, right?'

Luke hesitated, his gaze sweeping over her. 'Do you really think this is a good—'

'My terms, you said—' she cut across him, her voice hard '—didn't you? So why are you still trying to take control?'

He stilled. 'I'm not.'

'No?' She took a step towards him, amazed at how angry she felt. Not at Luke, not at herself for once. Yet she still felt it, that hot tide washing over her, obliterating any rational thought. 'All right, then. Here are my terms. Strip.'

He blinked. 'Strip?'

She nodded, her jaw bunched. 'Strip, Luke.'

For a second he looked as if he was going to object. Refuse. Aurelie put her hands on her hips, her eyebrows raised in angry challenge. She could hear her breathing coming hard and fast.

'Okay,' he said quietly, and began to unbutton his shirt.

Aurelie felt a little shiver of disbelief. He was actually obeying her. *She was in control.* She watched, her eyes wide, as he finished unbuttoning his shirt, shrugging out of the expensive cotton. She loved his chest. Loved the hard planes, the way that broad expanse narrowed to those slim hips.

'Your belt,' she snapped. 'Your trousers.'

His gaze steady on her, he undid his belt. Took off his trousers.

'Socks?' he asked, eyebrows raised, and she felt an almost hysterical laugh well up inside her. She nodded. Luke took off his socks. He only wore a pair of navy silk boxers. He waited, and so did she, because hell if she knew what she wanted now.

'Go lie down on the bed,' she said, and heard the waver in her voice. She wasn't sure about this any more. She'd started out angry and strong but now she just felt confused. Sad too, and dangerously close to tears.

She followed Luke into the bedroom and watched as he sat on the edge of the bed, swung his legs over. Lay down and waited, hands behind his head.

She let out a trembling laugh. 'You look a lot more relaxed than I would.'

'I am relaxed.'

'Really?' She sat on the edge of the bed.

'What do you want, Aurelie?' Luke asked quietly, and she knew, she knew that whatever she said she wanted, he would find a way to make it happen. He'd put himself completely in her hands, and she understood that that was what trust was.

Luke trusted her.

And she wanted to trust him.

'I want,' she said, her voice shaking, 'you to hold me. Just hold me.'

And he did, pulling her gently into his arms. She curved her body around his, craving his solid warmth. And as he stroked her hair she did the one thing she'd never, ever wanted to do.

She cried.

Sobbed, really, ugly, harsh sounds that clawed their way out of her chest and tore at her throat. She wrapped her arms around Luke and he held on tight as she sobbed out all the loneliness and pain and confusion she'd ever felt.

Just when she thought she might get a handle on it, she felt new sobs coming up from deep within her and after fifteen minutes or an hour—she had no idea which—she finally managed to wipe her blotchy face and laugh shakily.

'I'm a complete mess.'

'You're beautiful.'

She laughed again, the sound even shakier. 'You cannot mean that.'

'Don't you know by now I never lie?'

She tilted her head to look up at him and saw the truth shining in his eyes. 'How,' she whispered, 'did I ever deserve someone like you?'

'I could ask the same thing.'

She shook her head. 'I don't see how.'

'You're selling yourself short, Aurelie. You often do, you know.' Tenderly he wiped the damp strands of her hair away from her face, tucked them behind her ears. 'You make me laugh. You challenge and thrill me. You stun me with your talent and your courage. Of course I could ask the same question.'

She shook her head, still incredulous, and tenderly Luke

kissed her eyelids, her nose, and then her mouth. 'I do ask it,' he whispered against her lips and, without even thinking about it, just needing to, Aurelie kissed him back. Softly, yet with intent. With promise.

Luke hesitated, just for a second, but long enough so she whispered, 'My terms.'

His hands stilled on her shoulders. 'Which are?' he asked softly.

'I want to kiss you. And you've got to kiss me back.'

'Those are terms I can live with.' She felt him smile against her mouth and then she kissed him again, deeper this time, exploring him in a way she never had before, because she hadn't dared or dreamed of it.

Now she had the time, the desire and most of all the control to kiss him at leisure. In depth. She rolled him onto his back and propped herself up on her elbow, kissing every part of him that she wanted to: his lips, his eyes, the curve of his neck, the line of his jaw. His ear, his shoulder, the taut skin of his chest. She heard him groan softly and she felt a thrill of—no, not power. This wasn't even about power. It was about pleasure and trust and love.

His response made her own need flare deeper, and she kissed his mouth again, deeply, rolling on top of him. Luke placed his hands on her hips to steady her and as Aurelie pressed against him she felt that need flare again, white-hot, burning so brightly she couldn't think for a moment.

'Touch me,' she whispered. 'Touch me back.'

'Where?' Luke whispered, and she felt another thrill of pleasure just at the question.

She took his hand and slid it up along her side, placed it on her breast and closed her eyes. 'There.' And when Luke took that touch and made it his own, his fingers stroking her softness, she let out a shudder. 'And here.' She took his other hand and placed it on her tummy, dared to slide it lower, and another shudder ripped through her as his hands slid under her dress, edged her underwear aside. 'Yes…' She pressed against him as his fingers moved deeper, pleasure shooting like sparks through her whole body. There was a freedom in this, and a wonder. She felt a kind of amazed joy, that she could feel so good, that a man could make her feel so good. That Luke could.

'I want to take off my clothes,' she managed.

'With or without my help?'

She heard a smile in Luke's voice and smiled back. 'With.'

He tugged the zip down her back and she shrugged her shoulders so the dress slid off her. Luke managed the rest, and her bra and panties too. She was naked, and with one swift tug of his boxers he was naked too.

'There.' She spoke on a sigh of satisfaction and Luke smiled as he stretched out next to her.

'Now what would you like?'

She laughed, because it felt so amazing to be asked. 'Hmm…let me think.' She touched his cheek, his jaw, the smooth hardness of his chest. Slid her hand lower to the dip of his waist, and then slowly, wonderingly, wrapped her fingers around the length of his erection. 'More of the same, really,' she whispered, and on a groan Luke kissed her.

They didn't say much of anything any more; she didn't need to give instructions and he didn't need to ask permission. This was what sex was supposed to be, she thought hazily. *Making love.* Moving in silent and loving synchronicity, hands and mouths and bodies, all of it as one together.

And when he finally slid inside her, filling her right up, she felt a sense of completion and wholeness she'd never felt before. Never even known you could have.

Gently, still moving inside her, he wiped the tears that had sprung unbidden to her eyes, kissed her damp eyelids. Aurelie let out a wobbly laugh.

'I'm just so *happy*,' she choked, and Luke kissed her mouth.

'I know,' he said. 'I am too.'

Sunlight streamed through the bedroom windows, touched Aurelie's sleeping form with gold. Smiling, Luke rolled over on his side, smoothed her skin from her shoulder to hip with his hand. He loved the feel of her. Loved the taste of her too, the look of her, and most definitely the sound of her. He loved her, full stop.

It didn't scare him, now that he knew who she was. And who she wasn't. No, it thrilled him and made him incredibly thankful at the same time, because he was pretty sure she loved him too. He'd earned her trust. He'd won her love. He felt a sense of completion and wholeness that came not just from last night, but from finally, wondrously coming full circle after a lifetime of feeling only failure and regret. He'd made this right. He'd made *them* right.

Aurelie's eyes fluttered open and, still hazy with sleep, she smiled. Reached for him with such simple ease that Luke's heart sang. Who would ever have thought that it could be so easy between them? That it would be so wonderful?

'Good morning,' he murmured, and kissed her. She kissed him back.

A little—or perhaps a long—while later, they showered and dressed and ate breakfast out on the terrace overlooking Victoria Harbour.

'Look at this.' He'd been scanning the headlines on his tablet computer and now he handed it to Aurelie. She glanced at the article, her eyebrows rising at the headline: *Aurelie Returns, Better than Ever.*

'That was quick.'

He smiled. 'I knew they'd like the song.'

'That's just one article. There will be others.'

'Does that bother you?'

She handed back the tablet, a furrow between her eyes. 'It doesn't bother me, not the way it used to, when I felt defined by what people wrote or said about me.' She let out a slow breath, and he knew this kind of emotional intimacy was still new for her, still hard. 'It doesn't bother me because I have someone in my life who knows who I really am.' She offered him a tentative smile. 'I never had that before.'

Luke reached for her hand. 'I'm glad you have it now.'

'But I don't want a comeback. I don't want to be famous again.'

'You don't?'

She shook her head. 'Singing in public again was more for me than the audience. I wanted to...to vindicate myself, I suppose. But I don't want to be Aurelie again, not in any incarnation. I've had enough of fame to last several lifetimes.'

He twined his fingers with hers. 'And what if these concerts catapult you back into the spotlight?'

'The spotlight will move off me in a few weeks or months or maybe even days, when I refuse to give them what they want. More concerts, more tabloid-worthy moments. I'm done with all that.'

'You're sure?'

'Yes.' She glanced up at him, worry shadowing her eyes, darkening them to slate. 'Do you mind?'

'Mind? Why would I mind?'

She shrugged. 'I don't know. The fame thing, it's kind of big.'

'To be honest, I'd have a harder time following you around on a concert circuit, but I'd do it if that's what you wanted.'

'And what about what you want?'

'I've got everything I want.' He smiled and squeezed her hand. 'You sing this afternoon, and then we have two days until Tokyo. Let's go away somewhere, just the two of us.'

Her eyes widened, her mouth curving in anticipation. 'Where?'

'I'll surprise you.'

He chose an incredibly exclusive resort on a tiny island off the coast of Hong Kong, the kind of place reporters or paparazzi could never find. The kind of place where he could pamper Aurelie all he wanted and they could revel in each other, in long, lazy days on the beach and long, loving nights in their bed, or the hot tub, or even on the beach again. Everywhere.

The night before they were to leave for Tokyo they lay in bed, the sliding glass doors open to the beach, the ocean breeze rustling the gauzy curtains. Moonlight slid over the rumpled covers, their twined legs. Aurelie was silent, one slender hand resting on his bare chest, over the steady thud of his heart.

Luke brushed his lips against her hair. 'What are you thinking?' he asked quietly, because he sensed something from her that was thoughtful, maybe even sad.

'Just how I don't want this to end. I don't want to go back to real life.'

'I'm not sure I know what real life is any more.' He paused, thinking to say more, then decided not to. He hadn't told her he loved her yet, and she hadn't said it, either. He wasn't afraid of saying those three little words, but he wondered how Aurelie felt about hearing them. This was all still so new, and maybe even fragile. There would be time enough later to figure out how this—*them*—was going to work.

On the plane to Tokyo he reluctantly refocused on work. He hadn't given Bryant's or business a single thought in forty-eight hours, which had to be a record for him. Now he checked his phone and groaned inwardly at the twenty-two texts he'd been sent. Most of them, fortunately, concerned minor matters, but one was a tersely worded command from his brother Aaron.

Wait for me in Tokyo.

Irritation rippled through him. Was his brother actually going to fly all the way to Tokyo to boss him around? No doubt he'd seen some of the press about Aurelie and the openings and wanted to throw his weight around, as he always did.

'What's wrong?' Aurelie asked quietly, and Luke glanced up. Over the last few days they'd become amazingly attuned to one another. Aurelie knew him as well as he knew her.

Not quite.

The thought slid slyly into his mind. She might have completely unburdened herself, but in many ways—crucial ways—he was still buttoned up as tight as ever. He still had secrets, and ones he had no desire or intention to share. She had enough to deal with; she didn't need his remembered pain. He slid his phone into his jacket pocket, glanced away. 'Just work stuff.'

Twenty minutes later they landed in Tokyo.

They took a limo to The Peninsula, the luxury hotel Luke's PA had booked overlooking the Imperial Palace Gardens. The air was crisper than in any of their other destinations, a hint of autumn on the breeze that ruffled the leaves of the trees lining the street.

'I cancelled your hotel suite,' he told her as they checked in. Fortunately there was no message from Aaron, and Luke half-hoped his brother had decided to abandon the trip. He turned to Aurelie. 'I hope you don't mind.'

She smiled, eyebrows raised. 'Why would I mind?'

'You might want a bit of privacy.'

'I think a two thousand square metre suite should provide enough of that,' she answered with a little laugh.

The bellhop led them to the penthouse suite, showed them

all of its rooms and wraparound terrace. When they were alone Luke pulled her into his arms, kissed his way down her throat. He loved the feel of her, the sense of rightness she gave him. 'As much as I'd like to finish what I've started,' he murmured against her skin, 'you have a concert to get to.'

'I know,' she agreed on a sigh of disappointment.

He straightened, bringing her with him so he could look into those slate-blue eyes he loved. 'Are you nervous?'

'No, which is amazing considering how terrified I was a few days ago.'

'You've changed.'

'Thanks to you.' She smiled. 'I know I'm not going to get glowing reviews all around. Someone will hate it, and they'll make sure to let me know.' Her mouth twisted wryly. 'But it doesn't matter. It really doesn't.'

'I'm glad,' Luke said, and with one more kiss because he just couldn't resist he smoothed her hair and dress and they went to get ready for the opening.

Two hours later Luke was standing by the side of the stage watching as Aurelie miked up to go on. She wore a flowing dress of pale green silk with a gauzy overlay, her hair pulled up in a loose chignon. She looked effortlessly beautiful, wonderfully natural. His heart swelled with love.

'What the hell,' a voice snapped out from behind him, 'is she doing here?'

Luke turned around to stare into the furious face of his brother Aaron.

CHAPTER TWELVE

'HELLO, AARON,' LUKE said evenly. 'I think I could ask you the same question.'

Aaron just shook his head. 'What are you talking about?'

'What the hell,' Luke asked mildly, 'are you doing here?'

'Saving your ass. Didn't you get my text?'

'Last time I checked, it didn't need saving.' Aaron opened his mouth but Luke forestalled him with one up-flung hand. 'Be quiet. She's about to start.'

Eyes narrowed, Aaron closed his mouth. Aurelie started to sing, and Luke listened to her smoky voice float through the crowd, hushing even the tiniest whisper. Everyone was entranced, including him.

But not Aaron. The second her voice died away Aaron grabbed his arm. Luke shook it off.

'She goes, Luke.'

Luke turned around. 'What do you mean, she goes?'

'She goes. Now. The last thing Bryant's needs is someone with her reputation linked to it—'

Luke eyed him coldly. 'Aurelie has done wonders for Bryant's image, Aaron.'

Just then she came off the stage, her widened gaze taking in the two of them.

Luke knew he didn't want his brother talking to Aurelie. Aaron had the tact of a tank when it came to getting his own way. 'Just give us a minute please, Aurelie,' he told her, and he heard the suppressed anger in his voice. So did she. She tensed, her eyes going wide before she nodded and, still holding her guitar, walked past them to her dressing room.

'Let's take this somewhere private,' Luke said coolly. 'The *really* last thing Bryant's needs is two of the Bryant brothers coming to blows in front of a thousand guests.'

'Coming to blows?' Aaron arched an eyebrow. 'All over a woman, Luke? Didn't you learn anything from our father?'

'Aurelie is nothing like our father's mistresses,' Luke snapped. Not trusting himself to say another word, he turned on his heel and went upstairs to one of the corporate offices. Aaron followed him, closing the door behind him and leaning against it with his arms folded.

'I appreciate she's probably pretty good in the sack, but she goes, Luke.'

Luke didn't think then. He just swung. His fist connected with his brother's jaw and white-hot pain radiated from his knuckles. Aaron doubled over, righting himself with one hand on the desk, the other massaging his already swelling jaw.

'Damn it, Luke. What the hell has gotten into you?'

'I should have done that years ago,' Luke said grimly. He cradled his throbbing hand. It had felt amazingly good to hit his brother. 'You stay out of this, Aaron. Stay out of my personal life and stay out of the store.'

'The store? The store is part of—'

'Bryant Enterprises. Yeah, I get that. I also get that you've got to have your sticky fingerprints on every part of this empire, even though there's plenty for both of us, and Chase too, if he'd wanted it.'

'Chase,' Aaron answered, 'was disinherited.'

'You could have given it back to him. You knew Dad was just acting out of anger.'

'I wasn't about to go against our dead father's wishes.'

'Oh, give it up.' Luke turned away, suddenly tired. 'Like you've ever cared about that.'

Aaron was silent for a moment. 'You have no idea,' he finally said, his voice flat and strange. Luke turned around.

'No?'

'No. And the fact remains that you might be CEO of Bryant Stores but I'm still your boss, and I say she goes.'

Impatience flared through him at his brother's autocratic tone. 'Have you read the papers? Have you seen the positive press—'

'Yes, and along with the positive press they're raking up every bit of tabloid trash that woman has generated. Do you *know* how many photos there are of her—'

'Stop.' Luke held up a hand. 'Stop, because I don't want to hear it and if we continue this conversation I'll punch you again.'

'This time I'll be ready for it,' Aaron snapped. 'I don't care if you're screwing her, Luke, but she can't—'

'Shut. Up.' Luke's voice was low, deadly in a way neither of them had ever heard before. 'Don't say one more word about Aurelie, Aaron. Not one word.' Aaron remained silent, his mouth thinned, his eyes narrowed. Luke let out a low breath. 'Bryant Stores is under my authority. I've been trying to prove to you for over fifteen years that I'm perfectly capable of managing it myself, but you always step in. You've never trusted me.'

'I don't trust anyone.'

Surprise rippled through Luke; he hadn't expected Aaron to say that, to admit so much.

'Why not?'

Aaron lifted one shoulder in an impatient shrug. 'Does it matter?'

'It matters to me. Do you know how hard I've worked—'

'Oh, yes, I know. You've worked hard for everything in your life, Luke, always waiting for that damn pat on your head. You didn't get it from Dad and you won't get it from me.'

Rage coursed through him. 'That's a hell of a thing to say.'

'It's true, though, isn't it?' Aaron stared at him in challenge. 'You've always been working for other people's approval. Trying to prove yourself, and you never will.'

Luke stared at his brother, realisation trickling coldly through him. He didn't like the way Aaron had put it, but he recognised that his brother's words held a shaming grain of truth. He'd been trying to prove himself for so long, to earn people's trust as if that would somehow make up for that one moment when he'd lost his father's.

'I'll stop now, then,' he said evenly. 'You either step off Bryant's or I do.'

Aaron raised his eyebrows. 'Are you threatening to quit?'

'It's not a threat.'

'Do you know what that kind of publicity could do—'

'Yes.'

'You've worked for Bryant's your whole adult life. You really want to just leave that behind?'

Luke knew his brother was testing him, looking for weaknesses. He wouldn't find any. He'd never felt so sure about anything in his life. 'I'll leave it behind if I have to keep answering to you. I'm done proving myself, Aaron. To you or to anyone.'

Aaron's mouth curved in a humourless smile. 'Well, look at you. All right. I'll think about it.'

Luke shook his head. 'Forget it. I resign.'

'You don't need to overreact—'

'No. But I need to stop working for you. In any capacity. Don't worry, Aaron. I'm sure you'll find someone else to be your stooge.' Luke turned away and he heard Aaron's exasperated sigh.

'It's that woman, isn't it? She's changed you.'

'Yes, she's changed me. But not in the way you think. She's *believed* in me, trusted me, and that's something you've never done. And I don't want that pat on the head, Aaron. I'm done. I'm done trying to earn it from you or anyone.'

With one last hard look at his brother, determination now surging through him, Luke left the office.

Aurelie clutched a flute of champagne and eyed the circulating crowd nervously. She still didn't see Luke or the man she knew must be his brother Aaron. He'd looked just like him, except a little taller and broader, a lot angrier.

She took a sip of champagne, forced herself to swallow. When she'd walked offstage she'd felt the tension between the two men and she'd had a horrible, plunging feeling they'd been arguing about her. No doubt Aaron wasn't pleased about her part in the reopening galas. And as for Luke?

What did he feel?

She realised she didn't know the answer to that question. The last few days had been wonderful, but had they been real? You could probably fall in love with anyone in this kind of situation, out of time and reality. And she knew she must be different from the women Luke had known, those three serious relationships he'd had. Maybe the novelty had worn off. Maybe Aaron had made him realise that she wasn't really a long-term proposition.

'I should congratulate you.' She froze, then slowly turned to face the unsmiling gaze of Aaron Bryant. His assessing look swept her from her head to her toes and clearly found her lacking. 'You've managed to ensnare my brother, at least for the moment.'

It was so much what Aurelie had been thinking, what

she'd feared, that she struggled to form any kind of reply. 'I haven't ensnared anyone,' she finally answered, her voice thankfully even.

'No? It's true love, then, is it?' He sounded so mocking, so disbelieving, that Aurelie stiffened. Didn't say anything, because she wasn't about to give this man any ammunition.

And she didn't even know if Luke loved her. He hadn't said those three important words yet, but then neither had she.

Aaron shook his head. 'Be kind to him when you're finished, at least. He deserves that much.'

Surprise flashed through her. She hadn't expected Aaron to care about Luke's feelings. 'I have no intention of finishing with him.'

'No? Then perhaps he'll wise up and finish with you.' With one last dismissive glance, he turned away.

Aurelie stood there, her fingers clenched around the fragile stem of her flute of champagne, the cold fingers of fear creeping along her spine. She knew Aaron had been trying to get to her, to wind her up or put her down or both. It didn't matter what he had said.

What mattered was her response. It all felt so *familiar*, this encroaching panic, the ensuing clinginess. The terror that Luke would leave her, that she'd be lost without him. She'd lose herself.

She'd changed in so many ways, so many wonderful ways, thanks to Luke. But she hadn't, it seemed, changed in the way that mattered most.

She was going to lose herself again. She felt it, in the hollowness that reverberated through her, a sudden, sweeping emptiness at the thought that Luke might leave her. Maybe she couldn't do relationships after all. Maybe this was what would always happen with her.

Somehow she circulated through the crowd, smiled, nodded, said things, although she wasn't sure what they were. She looked for Luke and caught a glimpse of him across the crowded room.

He was deep in discussion, a frown settled between his brows. Aurelie stared at him for a taut moment and then, without thinking, she turned on her heel and made it to the safety of her dressing room.

She kept her mind blank as she threw her belongings into a bag and grabbed her coat. Her plane left for New York tomorrow, but she could go standby. Hell, she could hire a private jet if she wanted to. And what she wanted in that moment was to escape. To flee to a safe place where she could untangle her impossible thoughts, her encroaching fears, and figure out if there was anything left.

She slipped out of the store, hailed a cab to take her back to the hotel. She was still operating on autopilot, reacting as she always had before, and while part of her knew she should stop, wait, *think*, the rest of her just buzzed and shrieked, *Get out. Get away and save yourself...if there's anything left to save.*

She'd packed her suitcases and was just slipping on her coat when she heard the door to the suite open. Luke stood there, looking tired and rumpled, the keycard held loosely in his hand.

'Someone told me you'd left early—' He stopped, his gaze taking in her packed cases, her coat. He stilled, and the silence stretched on for several seconds. 'What are you doing, Aurelie?'

She swallowed. 'I thought I'd leave a little early.'

'A little early,' Luke repeated neutrally. He came into the room, tossing the keycard on a side table. 'Were you going to inform me of that fact, or were you hoping to slip out while I was still at the opening?'

'I...' She trailed off, licked her lips. 'I don't know.'

He stared at her, his face expressionless, eyes veiled. 'What happened? Did Aaron talk to you?'

'Yes, but that doesn't really matter.'

'Doesn't it?'

'No. I just…I need some space, Luke. Some time. I'm not sure…' Her voice cracked and she took a breath, tried again. 'I'm not sure I can do this.'

'This,' he repeated. 'We never did decide what *this* was.'

Was, not is. So maybe her worst fears were realised, and he was leaving her. Not that it mattered either way. This was her problem, not Luke's.

'And you don't think you could have told me any of this?' he asked, his voice still so very even. 'You don't think you could have shared any of this with me before you tried to bust out of here?'

'I'm telling you now—'

'Only because I came back early!' His voice rose in a roar of anger and hurt that had Aurelie blinking, stepping back. 'Damn it, Aurelie, I trusted you. And I thought you trusted me.'

'This isn't about trust—'

'No? What's it about, then?'

'It's my problem, Luke. Not yours.'

'That's a rather neat way of putting it, considering it feels like my problem now.'

'I'm sorry.' Her throat ached with the effort of holding back tears. 'I just…I can't risk myself again. I can't open myself up to—'

'To being mistreated and abused like that scumbag Myers did to you?'

She felt hot tears crowd her eyes. 'I suppose. Yes.'

Luke let out a hard laugh, the kind of sound she'd never heard from him before. 'And you say this isn't about trust.'

'It isn't,' she insisted. 'This is about what's going on in my own head—'

'You want to know what's going on in my head?' Luke cut her off and Aurelie stilled. Nodded.

'Okay,' she said cautiously.

'I've had a few revelations today. Starting with the fact that I've resigned from Bryant Stores.'

'Resigned—'

'My brother told me I was always trying to prove myself to people, trying to earn their trust. And he was right. I was certainly trying to earn it with you.'

'I know you were, Luke. And you did earn it—'

'Obviously I didn't, if you're trying to sneak away now.' Luke shook his head, his gaze veiled and averted so Aurelie had no idea what he was thinking. 'But this goes back before you. Way back.' He let out a slow breath. 'I told you my mother died of breast cancer, but she didn't.'

'She didn't?' Aurelie repeated uncertainly.

'She killed herself.' Aurelie blinked. Luke stared at her grimly, his gaze unfocused, remembering. 'I was the only one home. I'd come back from boarding school, Chase and Aaron were still at sports camps. My father was on a business trip.'

'What happened?' Aurelie whispered.

'She was hysterical at first. She'd just found out about another of my father's mistresses. He always had some bimbo on the side, which is why I've been a bit more discerning with my own relationships. I saw what it did to my mother. Anyway—' he shrugged, as if shaking something off '—she sat me down in the living room, told me she loved me. I'd always been the closest to her, really. And then she said she was sorry but she couldn't go on, dwindling down towards death while my father flaunted his affairs.' Luke paused, and Aurelie could see how he was gripped by the force of such a terrible memory. 'I didn't realise what she meant at first. Then it hit me—she was actually going to kill herself. She'd gone upstairs, and I ran after her, but the door was locked.' He shook his head. 'I tried to reason with her. I pleaded, I shouted, I even cried. But all I got was silence.'

'Oh, Luke.' Tears stung her eyes as she imagined such a terrible, desperate scene.

'I tried to break the door open, but I couldn't. I *couldn't*.' His voice broke, and Aurelie felt something in her break too.

'I believe you,' she whispered.

'In the end I called 911 but it was too late. She'd slipped into a coma by the time the medics arrived, and she died later that night, from a drug overdose. Anti-depressants.'

Oh, God. So much made sense to her now. She blinked, swiped at her eyes. 'I'm so sorry.'

'So am I. I'm sorry I've let that whole awful episode define and cripple me for so many years. My father blamed me, you see, and so I blamed myself. He said I could have saved her, that I was the only one, that I should have done something. For so long I believed him. I told myself I didn't, but inside? Where it counts? I did. I spent years trying to earn back his trust and respect. His love. And he died without ever giving it to me.' Luke drew a deep breath, met her gaze with a stony one of his own. 'I should have told you this before. I thought it didn't matter, that I'd put it all behind me, but I've been doing the same thing with you, haven't I? I even told you I was. I was trying to earn your trust. I was trying to save you and I can't.'

'I don't want you to save me,' Aurelie whispered.

'Then what do you want, Aurelie? Because I'm done with trying to prove myself. You're either in or you're out. You either love me or you don't.'

Love. She swallowed, her mouth dry, her heart pounding like crazy. 'Luke—'

'I love you. Do you love me?'

Yes. She wanted to say it, felt it buoy up inside her, the pressure building and building, but no words came out. She was still so afraid. Afraid of losing herself, giving up control—

'I see,' Luke said quietly.

'It's not that simple,' she whispered.

Luke stared at her for a long moment. He looked so unyielding, yet a bleak sorrow flickered in the dark depths of his eyes. 'Actually,' he said, 'it is.'

Without another word, he turned and walked out of the room.

The flight back to New York was a blur, as was the drive up to Vermont. Aurelie arrived back at her grandma's house twenty-four hours after she'd left Tokyo. Left Luke, and her heart with him.

She dropped her bags by the door and walked through the rooms like a sleepwalker. She'd only been gone a little less than two weeks, yet it felt like forever. She'd lived a lifetime in the space of ten days. Lived and died.

For she was back exactly where she'd started, where she'd been stuck for years. Alone, hopeless, unable to change.

Just the memory of the hard, blazing look on Luke's face as he asked her if she loved him made her cringe and want to cry. She'd been too much of a coward to admit the truth, to take that leap.

She'd failed him, and failed herself. Fear rather than trust—*love*—had guided her actions.

In her more rational moments she convinced herself that it really was better this way, that Luke would be better off with someone more like him. Someone steady and balanced, who didn't drag a lifetime of emotional baggage behind her.

Yet in the middle of the night when her bed felt far too

empty, when she stared at her guitar or piano and couldn't summon the will to play, when every colour seemed to have been leached from the landscape of her life, she thought differently. She thought she might do anything to get him back, to have the chance to tell him that she loved him and was willing to take that risk, that he didn't have to earn anything because she'd give it all to him, gladly. So gladly.

Two weeks after she'd returned someone rang her doorbell, which was surprising in itself because she received pretty much zero visitors. She opened it, her heart lurching when she saw the familiar figure standing on her front porch.

'Luke—'

'Sorry. I know I must be a disappointment.'

The man in front of her wasn't Luke, but he looked a lot like him. His eyes and hair were a little lighter, but he had the same tall, powerful frame, the same wry smile.

'I'm Chase,' he said, and held out his hand. 'Chase Bryant.'

'You like to cook,' Aurelie said dumbly, because she was so surprised and that was the only thing she could remember. No, there was something else. *Chase checked out.*

'I do make a mean curry.' He raised his eyebrows. 'Luke's been talking about me, huh?'

'A little bit.'

'May I come in?'

He sounded so much like Luke that her eyes stung. Wordlessly Aurelie nodded and led him through the front hall to the kitchen. 'Do you want something to drink? A coffee or tea?'

'I'm good. I know you're wondering why I'm here.'

'I'm wondering how you even know who I am.'

Chase smiled wryly. 'That part's not so hard. The fame thing's a bitch though, I'm sure.'

She raked a hand through her hair. 'Oh. Right.'

'I saw Luke back in New York. He's not looking so good.'

That probably shouldn't have lifted her spirits, but it did. 'No?'

'No. In fact, he looks like crap and I told him so.' Chase paused. 'He told me about you.'

Aurelie stiffened. 'What exactly did he tell you?'

'Not much. And not willingly. I've gone pretty emo since I've become engaged, but Luke's still working on getting in touch with his feelings.'

She laughed, surprising herself because she hadn't laughed for so long. Since Luke. 'So what did he tell you?'

'That it didn't work out.'

'It didn't.'

'Yeah, I kind of figured that one out.' Chase took a step towards her. 'The thing is,' he said, and now he sounded serious, 'I'm in love with this amazing woman, Millie. And I almost completely blew it because I was afraid. You know the whole relationship/love/commitment thing is kind of big.'

'Yeah.' She took a deep breath, let it out slowly. 'It is, isn't it?'

Chase smiled at her gently. 'What exactly are you afraid of, Aurelie?'

'Everything,' she whispered and blinked hard.

'Are you afraid Luke will leave you? Hurt you? Because that was my thing. But maybe yours is something else.'

She glanced down. 'I don't think he'll mean to.'

'But you still think he will?'

She looked up, her eyes filled with tears. 'I'm just so afraid that I can't change.'

Chase tilted his head, regarded her quietly. 'How do you want to change?'

She sniffed. Loudly. 'I was in a relationship before and when it ended I...I was wrecked. Completely wrecked. I spun out of control and I can't stand the thought of that happening again, of losing myself again—'

Chase laughed softly, a gentle sound without any malice. 'Sweetheart, we're all afraid of that. That's what happens when you love someone, when you give everything. If Millie ever left me I'd be lost, completely lost.'

'Then how—'

'Because,' Chase said simply, 'life with her is worth any possible risk. But I'll admit, it took me a while to realise that. And maybe,' he added quietly, 'it will be different this time with you. Knowing Luke, I'm pretty sure it will.'

She sniffed again. Nodded. Because she knew Luke, and he was nothing, *nothing* like Pete Myers. And she was nothing like the way she'd been with Pete. With Luke she was different, new, *changed*.

She *had* changed. Why hadn't she believed it in the critical moment? Why had she blanked and backed away, defaulting to her old self?

She glanced sadly at Chase. 'I think it might be too late.'

He shook his head. 'I was just with Luke. Trust me, it's not too late.'

Two days later Aurelie stood in front of the renovated warehouse that housed Luke's new enterprise. Chase had told her that after resigning from Bryant's Luke had formed his own charitable foundation. She'd been surprised, and also pleased for Luke. He had never seemed like he actually enjoyed working for Bryant's.

And now she was here in lower Manhattan, terrified. Trying to change.

Taking a deep breath she opened the warehouse's heavy steel door and stepped into the building. The space was basically just one cavernous room, with folding chairs and stepladders and sheets of plastic all over the place. A young, officious-looking woman bustled towards her.

'May I help?'

'I'm looking for Luke Bryant—'

The woman's eyes widened in recognition. 'Are you—'

'Yes. Do you know where I can find Luke?'

Her eyes still wide, the woman nodded and gestured towards a door in a corner of the warehouse. Taking another deep breath Aurelie headed towards it.

Luke's back was to her as she opened the door. He was scanning some blueprints. 'Is that lunch?' he asked without looking up.

'Sorry, I don't have any sandwiches.'

Luke glanced up, everything about him stilling, blanking as he gazed at her. Aurelie tried to smile. 'Hi.'

'Hi.'

She couldn't tell a thing from his tone. 'I like the name,' she said, pointing to a sign on the door. *The Morpho Foundation*. 'Reminds me of a really great date I went on, when this butterfly landed in my hair and I kissed a man and it felt like the first real kiss I'd ever had.'

A muscle flickered in Luke's jaw and he dropped his gaze. 'Morpho is the Greek word for change, and this foundation's all about change.'

She swallowed. 'Change is good.'

He glanced up at her, and she saw that something had softened in his face. 'But yeah, it's about the butterfly too.' He paused, and one corner of his mouth quirked the tiniest bit upwards. 'And the kiss.'

It was more than enough of an opening. 'I miss you, Luke. I'm sorry I messed up so badly. I panicked and I acted on that panic instead of trusting you like I should have.'

He shook his head slowly, and Aurelie's heart free-fell towards her toes. 'I messed up too. I should have told you what was going on in my mind. The stuff about my mother. I just hadn't put it all together until that moment.'

'And I was so wrapped up in my own pain and past that I didn't think about yours.' She managed a smile. 'I thought you had it all together.'

'So did I.'

'I'm sorry about your mom,' Aurelie said quietly. 'I can't imagine how hard that must have been.'

'It wasn't easy.'

'I like the idea behind your foundation.' She'd read online that the foundation would be supporting children of parents in crisis. Like a mom with cancer.

'You gave me the idea, actually.'

'Me?'

'I thought about how alone you were, at such a young age. If you'd had one stable adult in your life things might have turned out differently for you.'

She nodded slowly. 'They might have.'

'Anyway—' Luke shrugged '—there's a lot of work to do before this thing is even off the ground.'

'Still, I'm glad you're doing it.' They both lapsed into silence then, and Aurelie's heart started thudding. Again. She'd thought they were getting there, working towards one another, but Luke still looked terribly remote. He didn't move towards her even though she desperately wanted him to. She wanted him to take her in his arms and kiss her, tell her it was all going to work out.

She wanted him to do all the work.

And suddenly she got it. This wasn't about Luke having to prove himself or earn anything from her. She gave it all freely, because she knew this man, and she loved and trusted him so much.

'I'm sorry for walking out on you in Tokyo,' she said. Luke didn't answer. 'You thought I didn't trust you and I can see how you would think that. How it looked that way. But the truth is I didn't trust myself. I was protecting myself, because I was so afraid of feeling like I did before. Out of control. Lost.'

'You'd only feel that way if I left you, if I let you down.'

'No. I never thought you'd let me down. I just…I saw you looking tense and angry with Aaron, and I knew he was probably telling you to forget me—'

'And you thought I'd listen?'

'No. But just the possibility had me panicking, and that scared me. I felt out of control already, and I didn't want that. But the thing I've finally realised—at least I'm starting to—is that love *requires* a loss of control. A giving of trust. And I was fighting against that because it still scared me.'

Luke was silent for a long moment. 'And now?' he finally asked.

'I'm still scared,' Aurelie admitted. 'I wish I wasn't, but I am. This is all terrifying for me, and I'll probably panic again. But I know I'm miserable without you, and I want to make this work. I want to be with you…if you still want to be with me.' Luke didn't say anything, and so she kept speaking, the words tumbling from her mouth, her heart. 'I know I'll mess up again, and I'll probably even hurt you. We'll hurt each other but I won't run away and I'll keep trying to change. It's a process.' She pointed to the foundation's sign. 'A metamorphosis takes a little time, you know.'

'I know. You're not the only one who needs to change.'

She swallowed, made herself say the hardest and most vulnerable words of all. The most changing. 'I love you, Luke.'

He didn't speak and Aurelie felt dizzy with nerves. Maybe she needed to check her blood sugar. 'Say something,' she managed, 'or you might have to dunk me in the sink a second time.'

Luke didn't say anything, though. He just crossed the room in two long strides and pulled her into his arms before he finally spoke. 'I love you too,' he said. 'So much. I'm sorry I ever walked away from you.'

'I'm not,' Aurelie answered, 'even though these last few weeks have been hell. I needed to be the one to walk *to* you for once.'

'Well, now neither of us is going anywhere,' Luke muttered against her throat, and then he was kissing her and Aurelie felt dizzier than ever. Dizzy with joy.

* * * * *

Mills & Boon® Hardback

February 2013

ROMANCE

Sold to the Enemy	Sarah Morgan
Uncovering the Silveri Secret	Melanie Milburne
Bartering Her Innocence	Trish Morey
Dealing Her Final Card	Jennie Lucas
In the Heat of the Spotlight	Kate Hewitt
No More Sweet Surrender	Caitlin Crews
Pride After Her Fall	Lucy Ellis
Living the Charade	Michelle Conder
The Downfall of a Good Girl	Kimberly Lang
The One That Got Away	Kelly Hunter
Her Rocky Mountain Protector	Patricia Thayer
The Billionaire's Baby SOS	Susan Meier
Baby out of the Blue	Rebecca Winters
Ballroom to Bride and Groom	Kate Hardy
How To Get Over Your Ex	Nikki Logan
Must Like Kids	Jackie Braun
The Brooding Doc's Redemption	Kate Hardy
The Son that Changed his Life	Jennifer Taylor

MEDICAL

An Inescapable Temptation	Scarlet Wilson
Revealing The Real Dr Robinson	Dianne Drake
The Rebel and Miss Jones	Annie Claydon
Swallowbrook's Wedding of the Year	Abigail Gordon

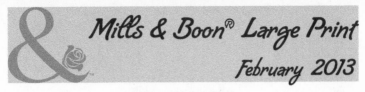

Mills & Boon® Large Print

February 2013

ROMANCE

HISTORICAL

MEDICAL

Mills & Boon® Hardback

March 2013

ROMANCE

Playing the Dutiful Wife	Carol Marinelli
The Fallen Greek Bride	Jane Porter
A Scandal, a Secret, a Baby	Sharon Kendrick
The Notorious Gabriel Diaz	Cathy Williams
A Reputation For Revenge	Jennie Lucas
Captive in the Spotlight	Annie West
Taming the Last Acosta	Susan Stephens
Island of Secrets	Robyn Donald
The Taming of a Wild Child	Kimberly Lang
First Time For Everything	Aimee Carson
Guardian to the Heiress	Margaret Way
Little Cowgirl on His Doorstep	Donna Alward
Mission: Soldier to Daddy	Soraya Lane
Winning Back His Wife	Melissa McClone
The Guy To Be Seen With	Fiona Harper
Why Resist a Rebel?	Leah Ashton
Sydney Harbour Hospital: Evie's Bombshell	Amy Andrews
The Prince Who Charmed Her	Fiona McArthur

MEDICAL

NYC Angels: Redeeming The Playboy	Carol Marinelli
NYC Angels: Heiress's Baby Scandal	Janice Lynn
St Piran's: The Wedding!	Alison Roberts
His Hidden American Beauty	Connie Cox

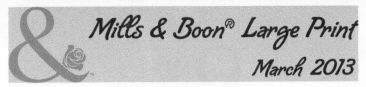

Mills & Boon® Large Print

March 2013

ROMANCE

A Night of No Return	Sarah Morgan
A Tempestuous Temptation	Cathy Williams
Back in the Headlines	Sharon Kendrick
A Taste of the Untamed	Susan Stephens
The Count's Christmas Baby	Rebecca Winters
His Larkville Cinderella	Melissa McClone
The Nanny Who Saved Christmas	Michelle Douglas
Snowed in at the Ranch	Cara Colter
Exquisite Revenge	Abby Green
Beneath the Veil of Paradise	Kate Hewitt
Surrendering All But Her Heart	Melanie Milburne

HISTORICAL

How to Sin Successfully	Bronwyn Scott
Hattie Wilkinson Meets Her Match	Michelle Styles
The Captain's Kidnapped Beauty	Mary Nichols
The Admiral's Penniless Bride	Carla Kelly
Return of the Border Warrior	Blythe Gifford

MEDICAL

Her Motherhood Wish	Anne Fraser
A Bond Between Strangers	Scarlet Wilson
Once a Playboy...	Kate Hardy
Challenging the Nurse's Rules	Janice Lynn
The Sheikh and the Surrogate Mum	Meredith Webber
Tamed by her Brooding Boss	Joanna Neil

)213 GEN STD LP